Grand

Finale

A murder in the Badlands

of West Virginia

by Joan Hall

ISBN 978-0-9819815-4-3

Olive Hill., KY 41164

Prologue

Carrie glanced at the clock when she heard a soft rapping at the motel door, 12:30 AM. Woody had left only 10 minutes earlier. He must have forgotten something. She rushed to open the door with one hand while with the other she clutched her thin nightgown together.

"Woody," she gushed. Her voice froze, then in horror, she screamed, "No, no." Desperately she pushed at the door, attempting to stop the masked intruder. For long seconds she heaved her might, but in vain. The broad, strong figure crashed the door open, sending her stumbling backwards. Her breath came in short gasps; panic weakened her muscles. She fell on the bed where she and Woody had made love earlier.

"What do you want?" She panted. "My purse? Over there, take it, please."

"You know what I want, Lola. You wouldn't give it to me so I'm going to take it." A voice growled with violent anger from a husky male form standing over her.

He had used her stage name, maybe he was a deranged fan. She struggled to get away from the dark hulking figure.

She noted he was wearing rubber gloves. He had plotted his crime. He was determined.

What had she done? Whom had she crossed? Whom had she pushed so far that he would violate her?

Her mind spun with desperate thought.

She knew men; they were her business. She could get out of this. "I'm sorry if I hurt you." She deliberately softened her tone but her trembling voice betrayed her fear. Her heart was pounding with it.

"We can work this out."

"No **we** can't." The mask muffled the man's voice. It was vaguely familiar. "I will work it out my way."

"You don't have to hurt me," she cajoled him. "I like men. If you know me, you know I can be bought." She attempted a light laugh. "Is that what you want?" Desperation grabbed her. She would say anything, do anything to save her life. "You don't have to rape me, just lay a bill on the table." The man uttered a guttural, throaty noise in defiance.

"Free, it will be free. Just do it and leave." Carrie steeled herself; she had been around. She had used her body for gain, but it had always been her choice. *I am tough and can stand a violation.* Tears threatened behind her eyelids as she spread her legs.

"What are you doing? No, stop that. I said you could have me." She fought uselessly as the intruder grabbed her wrists and pulled them up over her head.

My scarf, how did he get my silk scarf?

Quickly he bound her hands to the headboard rail, leaving her helpless.

Scream. She had used the wrong tactics, she thought desperately, *I should scream.* He must have read her mind.

As she opened her mouth, her breath was caught by a large hand, muffling her cry.

The hand held a rag. He crammed it inside, holding her jaws wide, gagging and choking her

A garbled sob was all she could utter.

She made a frantic attempt to kick him between his legs but he easily restrained her.

Submission, she thought, attempting a final ploy of letting her body go limp. The animal still held her down, rendering her completely helpless. He tore at her gown. The lacy fabric gave easily.

Carrie had always been proud of her body, had displayed it with ease on stage and off. Now she lay bared in shame, watching as her attacker pulled down his garments. He was already cloaked with a condom. He had prepared well.

When she felt him on top of her, she closed her eyes. She would escape in her mind. She imagined Woody and his arms. He always held her gently, even in passion. Did he know she was in love with him? *I wish I had told him but I was afraid it was too soon. In three months I will be graduated, have my degree. I can hang out my shingle. All this will be behind me and him. My life will be different. I just have to get through this.*

I'm a psychologist. This will teach me to be better suited to care for my patients who have suffered trauma. Carrie moaned when he thrust himself inside her.

She thought she had prepared herself for his entry. She had had many men but this was different. Each thrust was like a blow, injuring her wholly; mind, body and spirit, brutal blows that seemed to never end. *I will endure, I must endure.*

Finally he withdrew, leaving her numbed. Her body lay still. She squeezed her eyes closed, not wanting to see the beast above her. It would be easier for her to recoup. Then she heard a click. The sound sent a wave of terror through her. Her heart raced. No, no, he wouldn't.

She had cooperated, given him what he wanted. *My life, my life, don't take my life, please.* She moaned in an attempt to communicate. She opened her eyes to plead. Her gaze clashed with a cold hard stare.

A piercing pain entered her throat just below one ear and shot streaks of fire to her brain. She had been stabbed with a knife, and lay helpless with no defense.

"I hate you bitches, I hate you," he growled like an animal devouring its prey.

A searing, burning blade cut across her throat to her other ear. A warm liquid poured out over her shoulders and breasts.

Her brain grew foggy with pain but realization seeped in. Random thoughts flitted through her mind. *He is killing me. I'm dying. God, send someone to stop him, don't let me die in vain.*

Forgive me of sin and take my soul. I'm sorry, Juan, I failed you. So this is what it's like to die. No goodbyes, I just disappear, slowly disappear into a place of dark nothingness.

Eddyville Prison

Kentucky State Penitentiary at Eddyville, known as the old Castle on the Cumberland, was completed in 1886. The multi-structure complex is Kentucky's oldest prison and houses Kentucky's death row inmates and the state's only execution chamber.

Chapter One

Eddyville Prison
July 11, 2001

The long dimly lit hallway echoed the rhythmic clicks of my stiff leather oxfords as I strode the gray tiled floor. The guard at my side trod silently in thick rubber-soled work shoes. "Is this your first visit to death row, Reverend Daniels?"

I thought of what I had endured to get to this place. First, I had been frisked by uniformed officers with solemn faces, had my pockets emptied except for my driver's license (I was allowed to keep my pad and pen) then pushed through a metal detector.

I shivered. The passageway of cell house six seemed as cold as the hewn granite stones of the outer walls of Eddyville. "Yes," I said with a tug at my tight collar. "I've been with Trinity Way Church for about a month. My wife and I have barely gotten settled in. I assumed the schedule of the former pastor as soon as I could. I understand he, Reverend Joseph Roe, visited the inmates twice a month. Is that true?"

"Yeah, for all the good it did. The guard burst with a scathing laugh. "This is maximum prison, Reverend. These guys ain't your run of the mill prisoners. Drug pushers, embezzlers or the like don't make it to this place. These are murderers or murder/rapists like this animal you're about to meet today."

In spite of the cool temperature, sweat popped out on my brow.

1

I retrieved my handkerchief from the breast pocket of my suit jacket and wiped my face.

I had never before been called on to minister to inmates, had never thought about the possibility. My assignments so far had been in small towns where crime was running a red light and the nearest prison was out of state or at least out of mind.

"You're kind of young, ain't you, Preacher? You up to dealing with the likes of this place?" The guard gave me an appraising stare from squinting blue eyes. He was a boulder of a man, large head, thick neck, muscled arms and a long stride. I felt childlike with my five foot nine inch frame.

"I'm twenty-eight," I said. *I'm old enough to be more confident.* My hands were actually shaking. The harshness of the institution made me more than uncomfortable. The urge to run hit me, run from this dark confining space.

I was beginning to feel like a prisoner myself. I steeled my jangled nerves. The elderly Reverend Roe could handle this duty.

I could as well. I was willing to go to any length for my service.

"Well, we're here, Preacher, death row, the end of the world as far as I'm concerned. All the guys in this section will be put to death one of these days, I reckon. Have you seen 'the chair'?"

"Do you mean the electric chair?"

At the guard's affirmative nod, I said, "No, I haven't." My voice quivered.

"It's a nasty looking thing, located in the basement of cell house number three. The dungeon, I call it. That place is about as close to hell as you'll ever get on this earth. Of course the chair's not used any more, lethal injection is how they do it nowadays. We segregate the worst of the worst in three, locked behind solid steel doors. No visitors allowed, but I don't expect those guys would want to see you anyway. He laughed at his own humor.

"Man, I hate to pull duty in three."

He went on to explain the five custody levels of Eddyville, the general population wore khaki, protective custody were clothed in kelly green, segregated prisoners wore canary yellow, and minimum security wore dark green. I had seen a few of them out working the grounds.

"And then there are these fellows here on death row; they're garbed in scarlet red."

We stood before a massive metal grid door. The guard mumbled into a device on the wall.

A loud click resounded through the air. The portal hummed electronically as it slid open. We stepped through. The door closed behind us, sealing like a tomb. My heart picked up pace. Concrete walls surrounded the space where we stood. The expanse was broken with black iron grid doors. I was reminded of cages in zoos, where as a boy, I had observed lower life forms, like great hairy apes. Now, as then, I peered into the confined spaces to see what nature had mistakenly wrought.

Finally, we stopped before a cell. I cleared my throat.

"You can speak with the prisoner through the door," the guard said.

I noted the odors of the place, antiseptic cleaner laying atop a stale musty, closed-in stench. The only fix for the dank atmosphere was open air and sunshine.

Relief gushed through me. I wouldn't have to stand face to face with the criminal, and he couldn't reach me through the narrow spaces between the bars. I didn't like this feeling, very akin to fear. *God walks with me, I should never be afraid*, I reminded myself. This man I was about to meet was a creature of God, the same as I, and his sins, whatever they may be, were forgivable.

"Hey, Woody," the jailer yelled into the meager chamber. "You have a visitor." He stepped back allowing scant privacy.

I peered into the small cell. A figure rose from a cot and stepped cautiously toward the barrier that separated us. He was dressed in a red jumpsuit, the color reserved for death row inmates. His face appeared pale and gaunt and marred by scars from evident brawls, yet chiseled into striking features, like a model. His hair was jet black and his eyes were dark and brooding. He seemed no more than twenty-five years old at the most; not quite what I'd expected. I had prepared to do battle with the devil incarnate but I sensed no evil in the defeated face staring back at me. "Okay, who are you and what do you want?" asked a resigned, almost hopeless, young voice.

I stuttered, suddenly unsure of how to reply. "I...I'm Reverend Harley Daniels. I'm taking over the responsibilities of Reverend Roe."

The prisoner chuckled. I had amused him with my words.

"Is Harley really your name? Did your mama have a thing for motorcycles?"

"No, actually I'm named for my grandfather. My mother's father was named Harley. It's really an old name, going back for generations."

My response seemed defensive, even to my own ears. The conversation wasn't going as I expected. I glanced to the notebook I clutched in my hand. "You're Woodrow Howard Pierce, right?" My gaze flew back to his face. He smiled a half smile. He had been teasing me.

"Yeah , but I like Woody, so that's what you can call me."

"All right, Woody." I smiled; I was comfortable now.

"So, Rev Roe is really gone? I won't be seeing him anymore?" A hint of childish pouting lay in his words but didn't show in his face.

"Yes, he retired and moved to Florida."

"Florida. The lucky devil." The prisoner caught himself.

"I'm sorry, Preacher, I mean the lucky guy."

"I know what you mean," I said, visualizing swaying palm trees and a blue ocean. An uncomfortable silence fell around us. I decided to do my duty. "I'd like to offer you some encouraging words, Woody. You know God is there for all of us, all we have to do is reach out to him and ask him to come into our hearts."

"I don't know about that, Preacher, I think some of us are forgotten. In fact, I think God didn't just forget me, I think he actually turned his back on me, just left me to the devil's clutches." Resentment hardened his words. He reached out and grabbed a bar with each strong hand. "That's not a very good feeling, Rev.

I guess I'm just an unlovable cuss. Pretty bad, huh? Your own Lord rejects you. You know, I'm kinda anxious to meet the King face to face. I'd like to know why he had it in for me. What did I ever do to incur his wrath?"

The man's hopeless anger tore at my heart. Maybe the guard was right; I wasn't experienced enough to handle the duties thrust upon me.

I searched for words to aid this hurting man. "Is there no one to stand by you at this time? A family? Friends?" I was reminded of the youth of the prisoner.

"What about your mother and father?"

"A-h-h-h." Woody growled like a wounded animal. "I don't have a father, never did. I don't even know who the son of..." Woody caught himself. "My mom can't handle the situation, you know. She runs away from it. The doc keeps her medicated." He drew a long breath. "I can't burden her with my problems any more than she already is. I don't have any brothers or sisters. It might have helped if I had, you know, somebody to grow up with." He stared at me, naked pain in his eyes. "I bet you had a big family, didn't you? Brothers and sisters - the whole works."

Guilt coursed through me. "Yes," I said. "There are five of us. I have two brothers and two sisters."

"And a father?" he prodded.

"Yes," I said briefly. I could not dare relate to him the man of strength who had firmly and lovingly guided his five children to responsible adulthood.

"See," he grated "Some of us he favors and some of us he don't. The problem is, I don't understand why." He gazed at me with hard eyes.

"You're the preacher. You're knowledgeable in his word. Why am I being kicked around so bad?"

"This is a world of free will, Woody. You probably made some bad choices. That's what this world is about. If God laid everything out just like he wanted, this would be Heaven, but this is life, after death comes Heaven. Life can be difficult but God can help you through it if you let him."

"Yeah, yeah, yeah," Woody said in a deadened tone. He had heard these words before. With a shrug he turned his back to me.

"Wait." I couldn't fail, so soon. I had just met him. "Let's say a prayer. Maybe God will grant you peace."

"Okay, Preacher, say your prayer then you can get the hell out of here."

I lowered my head and struggled to find the words to speak to my master on behalf of the man behind the steel door. "Dear Heavenly Father, we humbly come to you today to request peace of mind for Woody. Help him to accept your will. Give him understanding, Lord, and strength to face the days that lie ahead. most of all, Father, forgive him of the terrible crime he committed against another human...."

"Hold it right there, Preacher." The words grated like steel on steel. "You don't have to ask forgiveness on my behalf for murder or rape. Don't you know I didn't do that crime? Haven't you talked to Reverend Roe about my case? He knows I'm innocent."

In utter shock, I stuttered, "Uh..no...Reverend Roe and I haven't spoken about you. I just have his schedule. He did note that his visits to you should be carried on. They seemed of great importance to him."

"His visits were important to me too. The Rev understood. He believed in my innocence. He knew the truth."

His words were accusing and I felt guilty. I hadn't bothered to inquire about Woody's case, knew absolutely nothing about him or the crime for which he had been convicted. All I had were the words from the guard - murder and rape. Who had been the victim? What were the circumstances surrounding the vile act? Suddenly, my mind was wrought with curiosity. I needed to know his story. Some urge from deep inside demanded that I hear his side in the matter. "What is the truth, Woody?" I asked.

"Ah, you don't want to hear the crap. Just go read yesterday's newspapers, they're full of it."

I didn't blame him for being resentful. I had not prepared for this meeting. I had fallen down on my duties. How could I bring solace to a man whose circumstances I knew nothing about? No wonder I had faltered for words. The seminary had taught me better than that. Without knowledge there could be no understanding or compassion. My human self didn't yet feel compassion for this person or his soul. Contrite and humbled, the tone of my voice surprised me. "I'm sorry, Woody.

Tell me how you ended up here on death row. I want to know." Maybe the honesty in my voice got through to him. He stared at me for a long time then he sighed "Well, the girl who was killed, we. . . we were kind of friends, you know." His voice broke and moisture dampened his eyes. He swallowed. "Her name was Carrie Ann Simpson but her stage name was Lola. She was a dancer at the Fantasy Nights club over the West Virginia state line in an area known as the badlands. She was a featured dancer, not just one of the girls. When the emcee introduced her, he said, 'There's a whole lot of Lola going on." Woody grinned. "She was kinda well endowed if you know what I mean, natural too, none of that phony plastic stuff. She was just as God made her."

I felt uncomfortable. A woman being described as a body brought a distaste to my mouth. "What was Lola, I mean Carrie Ann like? You said the two of you were friends."

"She was smart. She knew a lot about people, some kind of psychology stuff. She was always asking me questions, wanted to know what made me tick. She wanted to know about everybody. I think that was her undoing. She thought everyone had a soul. But Preacher, I know you may disagree, but there are some folks out there that ain't like normal folk.

They're just beyond fixing." He hesitated and his eyes stared into mine. Tiny bumps sprang out on my arms. "I'm not one of them, Reverend. I could never do what was done to Carrie Ann. Whoever killed her was a monster. I've done some stuff that I'm not proud of, a sinner through and through.

They're just regular sins Preacher, like drinking and carousing but never, never could I do a thing like that."

I felt assaulted. I was getting a view of an unfamiliar world, getting exposed to a person who appeared as a character in a bad movie.

But this was no movie. My stomach tightened.

"What happened to Carrie Ann and why were you charged? There had to be incriminating evidence, something that tied you to the scene of the crime."

"Yeah, you see, that was one of my sins; me and Carrie had a thing going, you know, we kinda loved each other. The night she was killed, I was with her and we had sex, so of course my DNA was all over her and my fingerprints were everywhere, on the beer bottles, the television. We had a bit to drink but I was never mad at Carrie like the prosecutor made out.

I was never in a drunken rage. We simply made love then I got out of bed about twelve o'clock and drove home. I had to go to work the next day. I'm a construction worker- a dozer man. We were in the Starlight motel in Jasper, Kentucky, a little town just over the state line from where she worked. She always stayed there three nights a week when she worked."

He stopped speaking abruptly like he had run out of words. I was lost in thought. I had no experience in such matters but his words had the ring of truth in them. Somewhere, deep inside, I believed him. Could there be such injustice?

Woody was waiting to be put to death by whatever means the state used to put their worst to death.

"So you see," he added in a calmed voice, "don't ask forgiveness for something I didn't do. I'll answer for the other things, but I'll meet the Lord with my head up cause I'm not guilty of that awful murder.

Do you believe me? Like Rev Roe? He knew the truth."

I had to reply and I had to speak truthfully. Always, I spoke the truth.

"Yes," I said. "I believe you."

"Well, now you can finish your prayer, Preacher." He closed his eyes and bowed his head awaiting my words.

I was unprepared so I lowered my head and awaited inspiration. After long seconds, words came of their own volition. "Dear Heavenly Father, in thy blessed son, Jesus' name, I ask you to look down on Woody in fairness. You are the Supreme Judge, Lord. Your will be done. Help Woody to accept that will. No one knows where or how he will leave this world. In his heart, Woody wants to come to you honorably, but it seems he is accused unjustly. If it be your will, Lord, find a way for the truth to be known so Woody can come to you at his appropriate time. I ask this in thy blessed son, Jesus' name. Thank you, Lord, amen."

When the prisoner lifted his head, tears traced the contours of his face. "Thank you, Reverend. Thank you for believing in me and thanks for talking to the Lord on my behalf." He stuck his hand through the opening. I reached out my hand for a brief shake. He turned away.

I felt dismissed and swung toward the guard who waited patiently.

The jailer shook his head "You believed him, didn't you, believed he was telling the truth.

I knew you were too young. Reverend, there's not a guilty man in this prison. Any one of them you talk to is as innocent as a babe."

"Really?" Woody seemed to me, to be telling the truth." We traced our steps down the corridor and waited at the secured door. "His eyes were so honest. My father always said, look into a man's eyes and you'll see his soul."

"You may have something there, Reverend.

I've looked into some evil eyes in this place. Some of them didn't look human. But I'll leave the guilt or innocence up to the courts. My job is hard enough without me going all soft."

"I understand," I said. The guard's duty was done. He had escorted me back to the administration office where we had met. "Thank you, Sir," I said and extended my hand to him.

"Any time, Reverend," he returned. "See ya."

I was escorted to the outside of the massive stone structure of Kentucky State Penitentiary, known as the Castle on the Cumberland. With anxious steps I strode down the thirty-six steps leading from the main entrance to the parking lot. I turned for a last glimpse of the gothic, medieval-looking fortress then I lifted my gaze to the clear blue sky of summer. The sun had never felt so good. I drew a deep breath. Woody would never again have the privilege of sunshine and fresh air. The prisoner's face hung suspended in the cells of my brain like the lyrics of a song you just couldn't shake. I envisioned his gaze. Yes, in my humble opinion, Woodrow Howard Pierce was an innocent man.

Chapter Two

I snuggled close to my sleeping wife. Beth had fallen asleep so easily. Always I had fallen asleep too, nestled in the cocoon of our love, our marriage and our comfortable bed. Lately though, my mind spun with ceaseless thoughts. Restlessness gnawed at me, robbing me of sleep. Most nights I tossed until eventually I fell into restless slumber, only to awaken at the first light of dawn.

I had an easy rapport with God, but I hated to bother him with such a trivial matter as sleepless nights. The cause had to be all the recent change in my life, the move to a new town, a new parish, new responsibilities, new people to whom I must minister, also visits to the elderly and hospitalized parishioners. My sermons seemed to meet with general approval if not enthusiasm from the congregation.

Surely my nerves would settle as I grew more comfortable in my duties.

I tossed to my other side, turning my back to my wife I thumped my pillow until it conformed to my head. I willed my mind still and waited for the relief of sleep.

Silently I counted the rhythmic ticks of the clock on the night table.

Twelve o'clock and I still hadn't fallen asleep. A sudden urge to speak with my father hit me.

He would probably still be awake.

He was my guide, always giving me sound advice.

Since he retired from Owensboro National Bank, he spent long evenings reading, a pleasure he couldn't allow himself during the years he was working long hours and raising a family. I slipped from the bed and closed the door behind me. I didn't want to awaken Beth. I would allow dad's phone three rings. If he didn't pick up I would assume he had gone to bed.

"Hello, Dad," I said to the familiar voice on the other end of the line.

"Hi Son, what are you doing calling at this late hour, it's after midnight." He hesitated then quickly added. "Is anything wrong?"

"No, no," I assured him. "I just couldn't get to sleep and thought I'd give you a call and talk for awhile. I was sure you'd still be up. What are you reading?"

"Oh, I'm reading the latest John Grisham novel. I really get into this law stuff. I'm fascinated by the workings of the court system. Mr. Grisham is an attorney, so he can tell it like it really is."

"You always did like a good mystery, didn't you?" Strange, how our conversation had taken an immediate path toward law. The prisoner I had visited earlier in the month came to mind. To be honest he had never left my thoughts completely, but hovered in a recess of my brain.

I fought against going to the small uncomfortable place but unwillingly I entered.

"Dad, how would you like to help me with a real life mystery with law and courts, trials, murder, prison, and a man named Woodrow Howard Pierce?" Relief flooded through me. I needed to discuss my visit with Woody. I wanted my dad's input. This was really why I called him, I realized.

"Is Pierce the inmate you visited, Son?" Caution tightened my father's voice. I recognized the tone he used when I was young, just before I or one of my siblings took the wheel of a car or before we left with friends to attend a party.

"Yes, he's on death row for raping and murdering a young woman but I don't think he's guilty." My words sounded naïve.

"He's been through a trial and sentenced to death. There must have been a mighty tight case against him.

Twelve people had to convict beyond any doubt." My father rationalized everything.

"I know, that's what is supposed to happen, but I think this time they made a mistake." Nervously I bit my lip.

"Well, that's possible, I've watched enough news expose`s to know that people are wrongfully convicted. Who was his lawyer?"

"I . . . don't know. I assume he had a public defender."

"Well, it's a terrible thing when an innocent man is put to death.

But, Son, what can you do? You're a preacher.

You don't know anything about the courts or laws or . . . anything."

"You're right." I agreed with my father. What could I do? "It just seems I'm being led to try to help the man, like I'm supposed to venture forward blindly. I have to try."

"Okay, Harley, I know you walk with God so I trust your intuition. Where do you start? Do you know anything about the prisoner?

Where he was tried? Where he lived?" Excitement lifted my dad's voice.

"No, no, and no. I know absolutely nothing but his name.

I'm sure he's innocent." I drummed my fingers on the arm of the sofa. Dad was silent. Finally, he spoke.

"There has to be a beginning point. Everything has a beginning."

A silence followed. I knew he was thinking, considering my best option, what I should do next.

"How about starting with Reverend Roe?

He's your one contact with the prisoner, and probably has enough information to get you started."

"Yes, the reverend had been visiting Woody for months.

He probably has a lot of information I need."

"Just what do you intend to do with this knowledge once you get it, Harley?"

"I honestly don't know. I may not be able to help Woody at all but I have to try."

"Be careful, Son. If this Woody is innocent that means a murderer is out there.

If you start stirring up trouble you could put yourself in danger."

"I've considered that, Dad."

"Your mother and I took care to shelter you kids from certain elements in our society while you were growing up.

We censured what you watched on television and at the movies. We made sure you went to a good school, and lived in a good neighborhood close enough to the city to be exposed to cultural events.

Remember our visits to the Owensboro Museum of Fine Art?"

"Yes," I answered, a warm feeling engulfing me. "The 19th century stained glass gallery is awesome."

"I think we did quite well, all our children are wonderful adults." I knew my father was wiping away tears.

"I know you did, Dad, and I'm thankful. You gave us a wonderful childhood, full of great memories."

"In retrospect, I'm afraid we may not have prepared you to deal with the likes of some people out there."

"Dad, I think you prepared me very well to cope with life.

By contrast, Woody was most unprepared. He had no father to guide him and he's in a prison."

"I hope you're right about this man."

"I hope I'm right too, Dad.

As I find out more about him, maybe the situation will become clearer." I yawned, suddenly feeling sleepy.

Funny, how a talk with my father always made me feel better, no matter what the situation.

"You should get to bed, Son. We'll talk again soon. Take care; I love you."

"I love you too, Dad."

Always, my father affirmed his love for his children. As kids, we sometimes grew uncomfortable when other youngsters were witness. But, thinking back, we were never teased.

Maybe, because Dad was there for our friends too, including them on fishing outings and ball games in the back yard. Mom always cooked enough to feed a few extra mouths that always seemed to be about. I stretched.

The bed seemed welcoming. I knew I would now fall soundly asleep."

The next morning, Beth was up long before me. The aroma of fresh brewed coffee wafted through the house to awaken my senses. I glanced at the clock. I had slept until eight o'clock; too late.

I never was one to lie in bed past seven.

Such a practice was never allowed in my dad's house, except on special occasions when late hours or illness demanded it.

"Hi, Honey."

Beth was already dressed and fresh from a shower. Her wet hair fell in ringlets around her face.

I walked up behind her and gave her a quick squeeze and placed a kiss on the back of her neck. "Stop that, I'm squeezing oranges, I'll make a mess," she said with a laugh."You were up late again last night."

"Yes, but I slept great when I did come to bed. Did I wake you? I thought you were sleeping soundly." I turned and leaned against the counter beside her.

"I always awaken when you leave our bed."

Beth gave me a sidelong glance from her green eyes; which were disturbed. My preoccupation with my duties was evidently having an effect on her.

"I'm sorry, Dear, I'm just having trouble falling asleep lately. It has nothing to do with you. Something has been troubling me. Last night I realized what I have to do."

"Want to tell me about it?" Her words were spoken matter-of-factly, but I sensed disapproval.

"There's nothing to tell actually, not yet anyway."

I asked myself, was I hedging?

15

"It concerns the prisoner you visited, doesn't it?" Yes, I had definitely sensed disapproval.

I glanced in surprise at Beth. Could I have no secrets around her?

Talk about a woman's intuition! "Yes," I admitted. "I want to do some research on him. I think he's innocent."

"Do you really have to? This thing about prisons and murderers and a low-life scares me. Such things aren't part of our world. Can't you have faith in the justice system?" A frown marred Beth's pretty face and the tone of her voice had risen.

"Justice is part of everyone's world, Beth. This is something I feel I have to do. Don't worry; I won't give the matter much of my time."

I changed the subject. "What are you doing today?"

"Janice and I are going shopping. I need curtains for the living room, something light and airy. I can't stand those heavy dark drapes another day. Reverend Roe had terrible taste." She gave a shudder.

"Great. Today's my day to visit the hospital. We have three members plus two others who requested my presence." I was grateful Beth had found a friend so quickly.

Janice was a church member and also on the board of directors.

She was an unmarried no-nonsense lady of about forty years who seemed to balance Beth's sometimes bubbly nature.

They were a contrast in appearance, Janice's thin figure clothed in dark, conservative attire verses Beth's taste of flowing pastels. A car honked.

With a wave of her hand she rushed out the front door.

By the time I had showered and shaved, the house was quiet. I carried my second cup of coffee into my study. I had at least an hour before time to leave for the hospital. I pulled open the bottom drawer of the desk I had inherited from Reverend Roe. I had moved all his leavings to the one compartment. He had given me a phone number. I picked through the sheaf of paper until I found the scribbled number. After four rings on the other end of the line a receiver was picked up.

A masculine voice, deepened with age, answered, "Hello."

"Hello, Reverend Roe? This is Reverend Harley Daniels. Remember me? I took your position at Trinity Hill."

"Yes, of course I remember you. How are things going?"

"Very well," I said. "I need some information...."

"Excuse me while I walk back to the patio," the old man said.

"The sun is so nice this time of the morning, gets too hot later in the day. A-h-h-h," he sighed. "Now, how can I help you?"

"The prisoner at Eddyville, Mr. Woodrow Pierce; do you have any information about him, like where he lived and where he was tried?"

"Yes, I had a folder on him."

His words brought a sigh from me. "I kept a folder or notes on most of my parishioners as well. Look on the top shelf of the study closet. You should find a box of records. I found keeping a file on everyone was very helpful. For instance, did you know that Mrs. Healey has four sons?

One, uh..., I forgot his name, is a researcher for the Institute Of Health and Todd, her second born, works for NASA. You can be a big hit with her if you occasionally inquire about their work."

"Thank you. I'll keep that in mind. About the prisoner, what impression did you get of him?" I hesitated for a second but I had to ask the question. I needed to know if someone else saw what I thought I saw. "Do you think he's an innocent man?"

"That Woody guy is a troubled young man. At times I was convinced of his innocence.

Other times he was so angry that I thought he might be capable of murder, especially if he had too much liquor.

Why do you ask? Did you visit him?"

"Yes, I did."

"How many times?"

"Just once, but I think I really got a sense of him. He did seem angry but rightfully so if he is innocent."

The Reverend paused and I heard him take a long drink of something evidently cool. "A-h-h-h. I visited a lot of guys in the pen, trying to save their souls but Woody is the only one I kept a file on. Something about him got to me. He never had a father which seemed to be a big issue with him and probably why I was drawn to him.

You see, I never had any children. I always wanted a son."

"Yes, having no father seemed to have been a big influence on how his life evolved."

"So, what do you want to know?" I needed to get to the point. The old man was tiring.

"Well, I suppose I need to know about his mother ...and where he was tried and...and stuff like that." My inexperience was showing.

How did I ever get the thought that I could be of aid to a prisoner on death row.

"He grew up in the eastern part of the state, in the mountains, beautiful area. Strange people though, rather clannish, don't take to outsiders." The reverend paused, I assumed to sip his drink. "I was moved to visit his mother, at Woody's request, of course."

My mind leaped with curiosity. "His mother? What kind of woman is she?"

"She is an attractive woman, quite beautiful as a matter of fact, not very old, must have given birth to Woody when she was just a girl. She's uneducated but intelligent and quite upset by Woody's circumstance. In fact, she collapsed during his trial and had to be hospitalized." The old man hesitated and sighed as if he had grown tired of speech. "It's all in his file. I made notes of everything I observed or learned about his case. I knew I was too old to be of any real help to the boy, but I kept his file, thought maybe someone might come to his aid. Maybe you're that someone."

"I hope so. Thank you, Reverend. I appreciate your help." "That's all right, call me anytime.

Like I said, everything I know and think about the boy is in his file."

After a quick goodbye, I hung up the phone. Anxious steps took me across the room to the closet.

The box sat on the top shelf just as the man said.

I tugged the heavy cardboard carton off the shelf and carried it over to my desk. Stacks of files filled the box to the top, each one with a name on a tab. The old man was a gem, I thought with a chuckle.

My attention was caught by a name, Janice Holland, Beth's new friend.

I hesitated, suddenly feeling like an intruder.

These people probably didn't have a clue about the practice of Reverend Roe. Just the thought of secret files made me pause. But then, I reasoned, the reverend had memory problems, these were just aids for his work. I opened the file.

Janice's file began with statistics like birthday, relatives, happenings in her life, but at the bottom of the page was a note. 'Janice is a troublemaker. She carries gossip. Her world centers on the church and its members. She needs a life.' I hesitated on a quick intake of breath.

The reverend seemed to be venting anger.

I probably would view Janice in a more cautious manner from now on. The files intrigued me. I gleaned knowledge about the members of my congregation that would have taken me months or maybe years to acquire. Now, when I gazed out over the sea of faces, I would know each personally. I would know their likes and dislikes, their dispositions, their faults, weaknesses and strengths.

Reverend Roe was a very observant man and thorough in his notes.

Finally, at the bottom of the box lay the file on Woody.

I lifted it out and lay it on the desk, then deposited all the other files neatly back in the box.

I reached for my mug of coffee but it had long since grown cold.

I read, Woodrow Howard Pierce, birthday 06-15-80, death row, Eddyville, born in Barton County, Kentucky to Summer Pierce, father unknown. Trial date- January of 2000. Attorney- Public Defender, Jason Watts. Verdict- guilty on both counts- murder first degree, rape. Currently under appeal. Troubled young man, angry at the world, but innocent.

Next were pages and pages of conversations from the many visits with the prisoner. The reverend must have taken a tape recorder with him to have been so through in recall of the exchanges. I couldn't put the papers down. Woody had spoken freely of his youth spent in a fatherless home which was a twenty-four by sixty foot trailer. I didn't understand his mixed feelings about his mother. He loved her but I sensed a distance between them from his words. The deep-seated anger I perceived in him came to light repeatedly on page after page. Could that relentless turmoil inside the young man have driven him to commit the most horrible of crimes? Suddenly, I wasn't so convinced of his innocence.

I unfolded a map, tucked into the file. A pencil line traced a line through the eastern Kentucky hills. At the point where it ended, a small x marked where Woody's mother lived.

I paused and wiped my tired eyes. The slam of the front door jarred me to the present.

Beth and Janice had walked into the foyer, their arms full of packages. My gaze flew to the clock on the wall of the study. The time could not possibly be noon. I glanced to the timepiece on my arm for assurance. The small black hands were both pointed directly at the twelve.

"Oh no." I had gotten too wrapped up in the writings of the former pastor. Was this a preview of things to come? I had let my curiosity about the prisoner interfere with my regular duties.

Dismay clouded Beth's face. She turned her gaze to Janice then back to me. "Harley, you're still here! Shouldn't you be at the hospital?"

"I . . . I'm afraid I lost track of time. Reverend Roe left this box of records." I couldn't explain my thoughtlessness. I felt guilty, as if I had perpetrated a crime, like I should be behind bars too.

Janice spoke. "Mrs. Arnold was due to have surgery at eleven. She needed your encouraging words before she went under the knife." Her face was unsmiling and her words were as sharp as the scalpel the doctor would use on Mrs. Arnold.

I dropped the papers I clutched in my hands and rose to my feet. "I'll be the first one she sees when she wakes up" There was nothing more I could say. I picked up my Bible laying unopened on my desk and strode toward the door, passing by Beth and the stiff figure of Janice.

Chapter Three

That following Sunday as I stood before the congregation, tension tightened my body. Several members' faces held open scowls and Janice sat with her arms folded tightly across her chest. She had evidently shared her knowledge of my indiscretion.

The chore of ingratiating myself into the hearts of a new congregation was difficult enough without the added stress of resentment. What a time for my mother and father to come for a visit. At least their glowing smiles lightened my spirit. Mom lifted her hand and lightly waved her fingers in encouragement. My sermon about forgiveness seemed appropriate on this Sunday. Regrettably, my experience had taught me that Church patrons could be quite unforgiving, demanding perfection from their pastor. My human frailties had to be masked, if possible.

I began my sermon. "My Dear Friends, only one perfect person has walked upon this earth and that person was our Lord and Savior, Jesus Christ, out Lord." I directed my gaze at Janice. She squirmed uncomfortably and dropped her arms to her sides.

"I'm sure no one here, especially me, has not made a mistake or two.

Can I hear an amen"

Reluctantly, it seemed the group responded with "Amens." I relaxed and continued my speech as I had planned.

"Good sermon, Son," Dad said.

He and Mom walked to the parsonage with Beth and me after the services."What did you do?" he asked with a chuckle. "That sermon was one big long apology."

"He forgot to go to the hospital for visitations," Beth answered for me, her voice tight and angry.

"I didn't forget to go, I was just late."

"Well, like you said, again and again, nobody's perfect," Mom said. We all had a good laugh. Upon reflection, the matter didn't seem so important. Beth and Mom went to the kitchen to prepare lunch.

"Come with me, Dad, I want to show you something." He followed me into the study. "You won't believe what the former pastor did. I grabbed the file on the prisoner and carried it to the sofa where Dad had made himself comfortable. I handed him the folder.

"What's this?" His lean face was quizzical. My father was still a handsome man and youthful for his fifty-five years. Just enough gray peppered his hair to give his a distinguished appearance. Often other women noticed to my mother's disdain.

He had had a minor heart attack, but got immediate care and received a stint. Mom still watched over him like he was her child instead of a husband.

"Information on Woody. . . you remember, the prisoner."

"Oh yes, Woodrow Howard Pierce. I've actually wondered about the guy after we talked. What have you learned?"

"Just what's in the file. Roe did all the work."

Dad began leafing through the papers. When he came to the recorded conversations, he leaned back and became absorbed by what was on the printed page.

"While you're reading, I'll get us something to drink." I walked to the kitchen and took my time squeezing lemons for a big pitcher of lemonade. Beth and Mom were deep in conversation about decorating the parsonage and paid me no mind. I carried two tall glasses of my concoction back to the study.

Dad didn't look up but reached out his hand for his glass. I sat down beside him and remained quiet and let him read. Minutes passed as he turned page after page. After he had drained his glass and handed it back to me, he lifted his gaze from the page.

"Well?" I asked.

"That boy's anger got him in a heap of trouble, didn't it? Couldn't the officials see he was just a troubled young man, not a cold blooded killer?" I didn't realize I was holding my breath until a long sigh escaped me. Dad was never wrong. To have him agree with my intuition meant so much to me.

"If there's any way I can help you, Son, I'd be honored.

I have spare time now that I'm retired although your mother keeps a tight reign." He smiled.

I thought, *he likes my mother's attention.* "Thanks, Dad. I'm sure there'll be ways. In fact, you can tell me what you think I should do first."

"Maybe a visit to his mother might be helpful. If you're serious about helping Woody, you'll need to get close to the person closest to him, and that appears to be her. Roe noted that Woody had no witnesses at the trial, no one for the defense to extol his character and even his mother broke down which couldn't have helped his case. Woody wasn't only mad at the world, the world was mad at him. The angrier he got the more anger he received. He started a cycle he doesn't know how to end."

"His anger is going to cost him his life unless I intercede."

"There has to be more to this situation than is evident. His kind of anger is deep-seated, more than not having a father. Although a father figure is of most importance to a child, especially a boy child.

Maybe the next time you visit the prison I'll go with you and meet Woody for myself, if that's all right with you."

"Yes, yes, I want you to meet him."

Relief flowed through me. I could do anything with my father's blessing.

Beth stuck her head through the doorway.

"Lunch is ready."

I saw her gaze rake over the pile of papers. I quickly shuffled them back into a neat stack.

"Great," Dad said as he handed me back the folder. "I'm starved."

"Thanks, Dad," I said. He smiled.

That evening after my parents left, I went into the study to put away the papers Dad and I had left on the sofa. I pulled out the map with the directions to the residence of Woody's mother.

Roe had not listed a phone number for her. If I was going to help Woody, I might as well get started. I picked up the phone and dialed information. Summer Pierce had no listing.

She either guarded her privacy or chose to live without the device. I glanced at the map again. The trip into the eastern part of the state would take about six hours. If I rose early I could be there by mid day and return easily by late evening. My Mondays were usually free of duties. I either spent my day puttering in the yard or catching up on other chores so tomorrow would be a perfect time to travel.

Strangely, I had spent my entire life in Kentucky but never ventured east beyond Lexington, a city lying in the center of the state, amid sweeping fields of million dollar bluegrass real estate. I knew nothing about my fellow Kentuckians who inhabited the Appalachian hills. A curious excitement swelled inside me like I was about to meet distant cousins, a people, whether by theirs or others' choice or by circumstance, remained isolated and separate from the rest of us.

That evening as we were preparing for bed, I said to Beth, "I think I'll head east tomorrow, would you like to ride along? The drive should be scenic."

"No." Beth's voice was firm. "I've heard nothing good about the area. Those people give Kentucky a bad reputation. Why should I want to go there and visit them?"

"Okay, okay, I'll go alone.

I've never seen that part of the state so I'm curious and anxious to see the area for myself. There's always been an air of mystery about the people who live there."

"You mean the hillbillies?"

"Beth, I can't believe you said that. You sounded so snobbish. You can't possibly believe those stereotypes portrayed on television. That is ridiculous nonsense. I've been reading about the area. There are many great universities throughout eastern Kentucky, graduating top scientists, engineers, leaders in every area of commerce."

"You're right. I'm sorry." She laughed."Go and enjoy yourself. I'll have plenty to do. I won't even know you're gone."

I was in my vehicle at five o'clock the next morning, a map and notebook on the seat beside me. For some reason I had picked up the habit of Reverend Roe's. I had learned to journal all my experiences. The first four hours were spent on familiar road and familiar land. I noticed a change about twenty miles beyond Lexington. The earth rolled into mounds and dipped into shallow valleys. Divisions of upscale houses were scattered about. I stopped at a McDonalds for brunch then pulled back onto the interstate, a cup of coffee in my hand. With my speed dropped to the minimum I could view my new surroundings. The hills grew higher and the valleys deeper. In places the highway cut through a hill. On either side of the passageway, towering cliffs stretched upward. At one particularly scenic spot, I pulled my vehicle off the highway onto the side. I stepped outside and viewed a bright green world. Hardwood trees on the hills were fully leafed. Winding around the bases was a narrow valley crisscrossed with white wooden fences lay a patchwork quilt made with shades of greens. I breathed a deep breath. The air was sweet with oxygen. A sensation filled me, like when I first saw Beth.

If she could see this beautiful country, I was sure she would fall in love as I felt I had.

Soon, I left the wide interstate highway and traversed the back roads. The next fifty miles grew more interesting. Each twist and turn of the narrow road took me deeper into Appalachia. More than once, I checked the map that Roe had plainly marked.

The road followed the lay of the land, winding around steep slopes and along ridges. The residences were modest ranches or mobile homes, occasionally an old two story structure with many rooms still stood. People of the old Appalachia were noted for their large families, some with children numbering fifteen to twenty. Our household of five youngsters sometimes had our mother in a spin. The parents of such large broods must have been strong people of both mind and body.

Finally, I neared my destination, Fox Hollow Road. I made the turn from a paved highway onto a rutted lane. Limestone gravel once layered the road but had been worn away or packed into the hard rocky dirt. Fox Hollow grew narrow. The hills moved in, allowing scant room for the roadway. A small rock-strewn creek traced along side the road. With the steepness of the hills, the small stream was sure to overflow with every rain; which probably explained the deep, pitted ruts in the lane and the reason all the structures were built at least a hundred feet up the incline.

Remnants of barns and cribs leaned against the hills like tired old souls, but were still functional, giving shelter to livestock and hay.

The farm houses that surely had accompanied the aged structures had all been torn down and replaced with narrow metal mobile homes.

The unattractive manufactured sameness had been softened. Individual residents had added porches, fences, and flowers. I slowed my pace and slid down the window of my car. Fox Hollow was alive with sound. Bird song filled the air; water gurgled over stones in the brook, cow bells clanged in the distance where cattle grazed. Numerous wind chimes, hanging from nearby porch rafters, tinkled. The air was rich and pungent with earth, woods, and blooms.

Finally, Woody's home came into view, a white mobile home with green shutters. I knew it from Roe's notes before I checked the address on the mailbox. "I hope she's home." I spoke aloud, testing my voice. I had been quiet for hours. An old Dodge caravan was parked under the carport. To have driven all this way and not be able to speak with Summer Pierce would have been more than disappointing. I might have even given up on this daunting task I had sat out to do.

A hand lifted back the curtains at a window and a face peered out briefly. I glimpsed long dark hair and a slim figure. Someone was home. I straightened my collar and climbed from my vehicle.

Chapter Four

I pressed the small black button on the door frame and waited. The door opened to the slim tall figure of a beautiful lady with pale skin, dark haunting eyes and a mane of hair as black as a raven's wing, which she had pulled off her face with a cloth band. She wore a simple white tee shirt above faded jeans but her clothing did not deter her beauty from shining through. Her features revealed the Cheyenne Indian heritage that permeated the area. Before I made my trip, I had researched the history of the people who resided in the hills.

"Hello," I said. "I'm Reverend Harley Daniels. I'd like to talk to you about your son, Woody."

"Another preacher," she said with a certain amount of disdain. "I don't see what good it would do to discuss my son.

He's already been tried and convicted." Her dark eyes were accusing. "Where were you and God when he really needed you?"

"Personally, I think he needs us now." I stood uneasy, first I straightened my collar then tugged my jacket.

She stared at me long and hard. Something stirred strangely in her eyes. "All right, come on in." She flipped the lock on the screened door and allowed me entry."

"Thank you."

"Would you like a pop?"

"A...a pop?"

"Yes. You know. . . . a cola."

"Yes, that sounds wonderful." I was thirsty.

"I took over Reverend Roe's position and his duties. I visited Woody."

I got immediately to the reason for my visit. "I think your son is innocent, Ms. Pierce."

"So?' She answered short and seemingly without hope. She pulled the ring on the top of the soda can and handed it to me.

"I . . .I would like to help him."

"What can you do? You're a preacher." I had heard those words before. "Please sit down."

"Thank you." I chose a worn tan chair close by the window where bright sunlight streamed through gauze fabric. She perched on the edge of a dark muted green sofa and opened a soda for herself.

"I have all the notes he made. He thought Woody was innocent too."

"Yes, he told me so but then he never did anything about it." She turned up her can and took a long sip.

I did the same. The bubbly liquid did taste good but immediately brought forth a burp. "Excuse me," I said, my face growing warm. She smiled. "He retired but he left all his information for me."

Summer's fingers trembled as she toyed with a strand of her hair. "I could do nothing at the trial, I just made matters worse. I tried to tell the jury that my son was innocent.

He could never do such a thing . . .but."

"I know. The strain of the trial became too much for you and you broke down. Reverend Roe told me."

"I failed my son when he needed me most." Her voice caught on a sob. "The court proceedings made me nervous. I just folded under the prosecutor's questions.

Woody grew so angry; he jumped up and yelled, 'Leave my mom alone. She don't know anything about what happened.' He would have struck the prosecutor if his attorney hadn't restrained him. He even called him a bad name."

"A son of a bitch?"

"Yes."

"He uses that a lot, doesn't he? Roe quoted their conversations in his notes."

"Yes, I could see the reaction in the jury box, the unsmiling faces and the arms folded across their chests. They found Woody so unlikable. I knew they were going to declare him guilty, and they did." She dropped her head into her hands. "He didn't have a chance. The whole trial was so unfair."

"I agree. He was not represented well." I hesitated about the next question I felt I needed to ask. "Why is Woody so angry? Lots of kids grow up without a father. That fact shouldn't be enough to cause such resentment in him."

"I don't know." Summer had raised her head and wiped her eyes. Her gaze avoided meeting mine.

I was always fascinated by eyes, truly considered them windows to the soul. This mother's were haunted with dark shadows of pain. She was hiding a secret from the world but not from herself.

"I tried to raise him well in spite of . . ." Her words trailed off as if she were about to say something she might regret. "I could have had an abortion, you know, but I didn't. I chose to give birth to him even though I was only sixteen and unwed. Twenty-three years ago, here in this part of the country, girls just didn't have babies without being married.

It wasn't easy either, my parents stood by me but never got over me having a bastard child."

My heart flopped in my chest. I was beginning to grasp the burden that had surely weighed heavily on Woody's young shoulders. He had carried a label, placed on him by the ones who should have nurtured and loved him unconditionally, protected him from such terms.

"Ms. Pierce, I know I'm being bold but it's only to gain more insight into Woody.

Would you please tell me why he has no relationship with his father?"

31

She folded her arms across her chest and a scowl darkened her brow. I had gone too far."You're getting too personal.

He doesn't have a father.

A man deposited his sperm inside me, that doesn't make him a dad." She sealed her lips like she would say no more.

"No, of course not.

Woody is so disturbed by the lack of a father's influence, I thought if he could meet the man who sired him, he might find peace in his identity."

"No. That is not your business"
 Summer pulled herself up until her back was tense and straight. "I've already said too much.

I love my son, but he's different from other people. I sensed it from the time he was a baby. He always misbehaved, always tried my patience.

I was firm with my discipline, but the more I tried to correct his behavior, the worse it got. He would deliberately do something to anger me then expect a hug."

I slumped in my chair. Summer had unconsciously revealed to me more than I had anticipated. I understood Woody. His mother had given birth too young, to an unwanted child, a child she thought of as different. I was not so far from youth to remember the comfort of a mother's embrace. To be denied that and a father too would have dire effects even on the best of children. *Poor little boy child,* I thought.

I hesitated but I had to ask the question. "Ms. Pierce, do you believe in your son's innocence?"

My words made her uncomfortable. She dropped her gaze. "I know he's innocent." Her voice was firm but her actions were more telling. She was not sure of her son's actions. "I've already given Reverend Roe all the information I had about the crime Woody was accused of doing. That's all I can do."

"Yes, I have his notes. I know the name of the victim, where the crime was committed and facts about the trial."

She rose to her feet, dismissing me. "Thank you for coming, Reverend. I hope you can help my son. I do love him dearly."

"I'm sure you love him very much, Ms. Pierce." I replied. I folded my notebook and rose to leave.

A knock on the door halted my words of goodbye. "Summer, it's Howard." A gruff male voice called through the screen door. "I've got what you needed from the grocery store."

"Thank you." I reached out and gave her slim hand a slight shake. "I really do intend to help Woody."

At the door stood a tall man with a large build. His face was kind. Gray frosted his dark hair, aging his still youthful appearance. "Hi, Howard," Summer said as she pushed open the door then took the brown paper sack from his hands. His gaze turned to me. "This is Reverend . . . " She stumbled over my name.

I stretched out my hand for a shake. "I'm Reverend Harley Daniels."

"Howard James," he said, grasping my hand.

He had a familiar air about him. "Have we met before?"

"No, I'm sure I would have remembered. I hear that a lot. I'm such an average John, I remind everyone of somebody." He chuckled.

"Thanks for dropping these off," Summer said as she deposited the bag on the kitchen counter.

The man's gaze questioned me.

"I'm here about her son. I was just leaving."

"Would you like to come inside, Howard?" Summer asked as she put away the grocery items.

"Not today. The boys at the station are swamped, so I'm going to help out for awhile."

"Where's the best place to get gas around here?

I need a fill-up before I head home." I spoke to the gentleman as we stepped from the porch together.

"Just follow me," he said. "I have a garage and service station in Paxton. We'll take care of you."

I checked my map as he turned his pickup truck.

Paxton was not on my return route. I had intended to retrace my path back to US 60.

The town was only a slight detour and shouldn't affect my schedule so I followed him. Fifteen minutes later I pulled into an upscale service station, a large white stone structure with four bays for vehicle repair and four shiny new gas pumps, seeming out of place in the small rural community.

Howard jumped from his truck and rushed over to me. "What grade would you like?"

"Plus," I returned. He seemed anxious to please. I had grown used to self service and stood ill at ease while the man did the menial task. I studied him. He appeared about Summer's age, trim but still muscular. I couldn't imagine why he seemed familiar. I had never met the man before.

"You're here about Woody?" he asked, keeping his gaze on the flashing numbers on the gas pump.

"Yes, I visited him and am convinced he's innocent.

I'm not sure I can help him."My determination was wavering. What did I think I could accomplish? I was just a preacher.

"I'd like to talk to you for a bit if you don't mind." He hung up the gas nozzle. "Come on inside." I handed him the forty it took to fill my SUV gas tank. This little foray into Appalachia was getting expensive, my second fill-up. "I thought I could give you some insight about Woody's upbringing, if you like."

"Yes." I answered quickly. I had been faltering in my resolve. His words renewed my interest.

"Summer and I used to date when we were kids.

I swear I loved her then and I love her now but crazy things happened and we were both too young to cope." He broke away from his subject and asked, "Would you like a pop?"

I rubbed my hand over my middle.

Could I handle another carbonated beverage? "Yes," I said. I took my can of soda and sat down on a straight back wooden chair as he had done.

Howard swiped his hand across his face. "I swear I would have married Summer if I had known she was pregnant, nothing would have mattered. If she had just told me, everything would have been different."

I almost choked on my drink. "You mean you're Woody's father? His middle name is Howard."

"No, no." His voice raised in objection. "Summer was raped. She was walking home, down a country lane. She had been to the grocery store. It was late in the day, dusky dark. Some guy jumped out of the brush and slapped his hand over her mouth and drug her back into the brush. She was small and had no chance of fighting him off. Nobody knows who did it. That's why she would never reveal to Woody the identity of his father. But I'm proud she gave her son my name."

My stomach tightened. Pieces of a puzzle were fitting together. Woody was a bright young man. Now I understood. He had to have sensed his mother's feelings. To be denied a mother's love could have caused irreparable harm. No wonder he was angry.

"Maybe I'd better start at the beginning.

Summer and I had been dating a few months. She was fifteen and I was seventeen. I really loved her and when we were older, I planned on asking her to marry me. Then, all at once, she changed, said she didn't want to see me and refused my phone calls. I didn't understand. I was hurt. I thought she had found someone else. I was so distraught I left Kentucky and went to live with my aunt and uncle in Indiana. I turned eighteen at the time so I got a job at a paper factory and stayed.

A couple of years later I met my former wife, Adriane. We married and had our beautiful daughter, Cindy. Meanwhile I heard Summer had a son. I figured the guy she loved just cut out on her and left her with a baby. Years later I heard about the rape but it was too late for Summer and me. I had a family and a job."

"What happened? You're evidently living here now."

"Yeah." He breathed a long sigh. "My wife and I split up. We both tried, we really did, for our daughter's sake. But when Cindy went off to college, her mother and I divorced. There was nothing left between us. We remain friends though. I took an early retirement, came back here and invested in a garage. It's doing pretty good too. You just can't find a good mechanic anymore, except here at Howard's Place."

He gave a wide smile then continued. "I've only been here a year so Woody had just been convicted. I didn't get to attend the trial. I visited him once with Summer. The drive to Eddyville is just too much for her. It's a sad situation." Howard drained his Coke and sat rolling the can between his big hands.

"Maybe Summer should receive some counseling. There are some wonderful agencies now that specialize in such matters."

"No, I suggested that. She's afraid Woody will find out he's the product of rape."

"I'm afraid he already knows," I said. "At least he knows a barrier lies between him and his mother."

Howard's eyes were troubled as he gazed into mine. "That would explain his behavior, wouldn't it? I raised a daughter so I know how it is with kids. Nothing is as important as giving them love and more love. Do you think it's too late for him and Summer?"

"I don't know," I admitted. "I hope not." I stood and shook Howard's hand. "Thanks, you've been a big help." I handed him my business card and he in turn gave me his. "I'll be in touch if anything develops." As an afterthought, I added. "Please try to convince Summer to seek council."

"I will, and I'll remain patient. I'll not leave her this time."

My heart ached for the child Woody had been. His mother, though well meaning, had treated him like the product of a rape, pretending everything was right and normal, yet always holding back, maintaining a distance, giving him signals that he was different but not revealing what that difference had been. How could people's lives get so complicated? Woody needed to know about the circumstance of his

36

conception but I couldn't be the one to tell him. That information would have to come from his mother. I needed to talk to Dad about this development. I needed his wisdom about my future actions.

Chapter Five

Tiredness consumed me. The long drive back home seemed to take twice as long as the trip that morning. Dusk had settled when I pulled into our driveway. Lamplight shone in welcome through the windows of the parsonage. I sighed. The day had been full of discovery but it felt good to be home. Beth would have kept dinner warm for me to enjoy. A good hot meal followed by a hot shower and an early retirement was my plan. "Beth, I'm home," I called as I hung my keys on a peg by the kitchen door.

She rushed into the room. Her hair was all mussed from running her hands through it. "It's about time you got here," she cried. "Why didn't you take the cell phone with you?"

I had forgotten the new phone, was not used to the convenience. "What's wrong?" I got a sense of dread in the pit of my stomach. My first concern was the family. "My parents?"

"No, they're fine. Janice's father had a heart attack and died.

She went over to his house at eleven to check on him as usual and found him there...dead, sitting in his favorite chair."

A feeling of relief flooded me followed closely by sorrow for Janice. "I'm sorry."

"Sorry! I should think you'd be sorry." Beth's eyes grew wide with anger and her cheeks bloomed with color.

"You should have been here or at least have taken the phone so you could be reached. We're not getting off on a very good footing with the congregation, Harley." She stood with her arms folded across her chest and her mouth was drawn down at the corners. Her anger tonight would not be easily appeased.

"Beth, be reasonable, I couldn't have known Mr. Holland would suffer a heart attack, and I'm always free on Monday to do as I please. The church committee gave that to me. I'm sorry for Janice. I'll call her after I eat dinner. What are we having?"

"Nothing."

"Nothing?"

"I spent the afternoon trying to console Janice. I went with her to the funeral home to make arrangements. We were both too upset to cook so we ate at Rosie's Cafe in town."

"Oh, I see." Emptiness gnawed at my stomach, a void that food alone couldn't fill. Beth and I wouldn't have our usual rapport at the supper table. "I'll see what's in the refrigerator." This was not the welcome I had anticipated. Beth and I were to sit down at our small kitchen table and I would tell her about all I had seen and experienced today. tell her of my discoveries and the interesting people I had met.

I found a carton of frozen lasagna and a couple of French rolls and stuck them in the microwave. I would eat alone. I had learned early in our marriage that when Beth was angry, I was best served to stay out of her way. Eventually her ire would cool. I ate my meal alone and in silence. My thoughts were troubling. My every attempt to come to the prisoner's aid evoked some type of crisis. Was this a sign I shouldn't continue with my efforts?

Was God telling me to abandon the task? No, in my heart I would know if that was the case.

I dreaded the phone call I would have to make to Janice. I was beginning to feel defensive when I thought of the woman. I shouldn't have to explain my absence today. I had a life and duties outside the church. I would not apologize to her for circumstances beyond my control. If I had been here, I would have tried to be of comfort.

In all honesty Beth was probably more able than I to console Janice in her loss. After all, she was her friend.

Sometimes being a pastor weighted heavily on my shoulders, weighty enough to make me stumble.

With a grimace and a long breath, I dialed Janice's number. I turned to see Beth standing in the next room. She was easily in a position to hear my every word.

I lifted my voice slightly as I conveyed my regrets to the woman on the other end of the line. We set a time for a wake.

We also discussed details of a funeral for her father then I hung up.

"Well, I've taken care of that," I said to my wife.

"Was she angry?"

"I really couldn't tell. Are you still angry? I turned the question on Beth.

"I'm not mad It's just that I like living here. I like the parsonage, the congregation and the town. I want to stay here and maybe raise a family. There are nice schools, a great mall and restaurants and low crime." I want them to like us. Beth ended by giving me a pointed gaze, then turned her back on me and left the room.

Her reference, I knew was because of my involvement in Woody's case. As much as I loved Beth, I couldn't let her dictate my life. I could not and would not turn from my responsibility.

Unless, of course, I felt it deemed by God "I think I'll retire early. The drive today was more tiring than I imagined."

Beth had to be curious about my encounters today, but I wasn't about to volunteer information. I would wait until she was in a more receptive mood.

"I'm tired too. Janice's situation has been emotionally draining. I think I'll join you." Beth stretched and I felt my heart stir as I watched her. When we married we vowed never to go to bed angry with one another. I had kept that vow. I was never angry with Beth, but her temperament reflected the fiery color of her hair and flared easily. I could apologize as I had done many times before and maybe she would fall asleep in my arms. But tonight I felt I was the wronged.

For once I should receive the apology. Beth lay on her side of the bed and I on mine. After awhile she spoke. "Did you meet Woody's mother today?"

"Yes, I answered. "Her name is Summer, Summer Pierce."

"Geez, only in eastern Kentucky would you find a person with a stupid name like Summer."

No, there would be no apologies tonight. I had thought Summer a beautiful name and matched perfectly the woman to whom it belonged. Beth didn't see beauty as I did. The world was filled with beauty. People were beautiful in every size and color. Youth was beautiful, innocence was beautiful, age was beautiful and eastern Kentucky people and their dialect was beautiful.

From this day forward, a cola would always be a pop. My rambling thoughts ceased abruptly as sleep seized my tired brain.

The next days were busy with preparations for the funeral.

Beth became her normal self. The anger she expressed on Monday seemed to be forgotten. Janice appeared to take the death of her father well. She cried but held herself in quiet reserve. Once I caught her staring at me across the crowded room at the wake. Coolness permeated her gaze, but softened when Beth approached to stand at her side.

By Friday things had settled back to a more normal routine. I could finally allow my mind to review Monday's experiences. I waited until Beth retired to give my father a call. When he answered with the familiar greeting, I burst forth words I had been holding in reserve for a week.

"Dad, I had to talk to you. You won't believe what I learned about Woody's past. I know why he's angry. It's a bad situation, totally beyond his control or mine. I don't know what to do for him. I'm stuck, Dad."

"Slow down, Harley."

I realized I had been gushing my words, pouring them like water from a spigot.

"I'm sorry, but Monday was such an exciting day."

"Well, I've got plenty of time, so relate to me all that you learned."

"Okay."

I took a deep breath and began. "Woody's birth was the product of rape."

"Oh." Dad groaned. "I was afraid this was going to get complicated. Go on, tell me everything, Harley."

I conceded and began at the beginning of the day. I relived my trip, sharing the highs and lows. I described in detail the woman with the beautiful name, who had intrigued me with her haunted eyes and the fatherly figure who was her protector. I repeated our conversations.

Dad listened quietly and when I was through, he sighed and said, "This boy needs our help. I'm with you in this."

His voice rose slightly, "I also have something to tell you."

"What?" I knew by the tone of my father's voice that something special was about to be revealed. "You know my friend, Mel Blanton, the guy with whom I golf."

"Yes, the retired postal worker."

"Well, his wife is a court reporter here in Owensboro. I requested a favor and she pulled some strings."

"And?" I urged my father. He was speaking too slowly.

"I got the transcript of Woody's murder trial."

I couldn't believe my ears. "Wow," was all I could say.

"I've been studying the transcript for days. The more I read, the more convinced I am of his innocence. I don't think he had proper council. The public defender didn't like his client. He should never have allowed Woody to act the way he did at his trial.

He allowed Woody to hang himself.

It's a shame but easy grounds for an appeal, in my opinion."

"You're a great help, Dad. I don't know if I could carry on without you."

"I'm glad to help. You know, I've kind of been at loose ends since I retired. I'll bring you the transcript tomorrow. Oh, and if you don't mind, I'd like to go with you to the prison on your next visit so I can meet this young man for myself."

"Thanks, Dad, I'd like that. I'll call the prison and make arrangements for a personal meeting. That would be much better than communicating through his cell door. I'll let you know when I can get an appointment."

"All right, Son, see you tomorrow."

Dad and Woody would meet. Now I would know for sure if the prisoner was guilty. Dad would know. He would be able to tell just by looking at him. That's the way my father was. He had an insight that I hoped I had inherited.

My mind raced. He would bring the transcript tomorrow. If I worked late tonight, I could free my time tomorrow. I still had to write my Sunday sermon and at five o'clock I had to council the church's youth group and Beth always expected to eat dinner out on Friday.

If only I had been as ingenious as the former Reverend Roe, who kept records of everything, even his sermons. I had found them all, years of them, piled in the study closet. If I had been as resourceful, I would have saved my sermons from my former parish. I had put a lot of time and thought into my work and then casually tossed it away.

I pulled forward the legal pad that lay on my desk then grabbed a pen then waited for my excited brain to settle and bring forth words. *My friends, my sermon today is about.....*

I struggled, then waited for inspiration, then struggled more. Maybe I would address grief and dying; the process of life. That would be timely since Janice had lost her father only days ago. I tapped my pen on the dark wood as minutes passed. For the first time in my short career, I felt speechless. A sudden thought seized me. Reverend Roe had a lifetime of sermons stashed in the closet. No, I recoiled at the idea. I could not plagiarize another man's work.

Beth called from the doorway, "Dear, it's almost five o'clock. The youth group will be here soon. I'm going to get in the shower. Where are we eating tonight?" The afternoon had slipped away.

"Oh, you pick the place," I responded.

"Let's try the new Italian restaurant. I've heard the pasta is great."

"Fine." I sighed and walked over to stand before the open closet. Reverend Roe's works were stacked in boxes on the floor.

I would just use his sermons for inspiration. The boxes were dated. I would go way back. The year, 1986 seemed a good selection. I had been only fourteen years old. Randomly, I selected a text. I couldn't believe my eyes. It was meant to be.

Reverend Roe had written eloquently on the death of a loved one. He had said everything I could wish to say. I would need to change very little of the speech to make it appropriate for today.

I hurried to my computer. I could have my sermon done by five. With only a slight hesitation, I began my version of the sermon.

Chapter Six

Dad arrived early the next morning. The box he carried in the trunk of his car was huge. "Is that the transcript"? I asked.

"Yes," he said, "hundreds of pages, interesting stuff. I was up half the night reading. There's a couple of odd witnesses I'd like you to take note of, a Mr. Wade Adkins, who owns and operates the motel where Carrie was killed and an Eric Jordan, who bounces at the Fantasy Nights club. I think they're both suspicious characters.

That little Miss Shapely Shaw, who was a dancer with Carrie didn't seem to me to be as good a friend to Carrie as she pretended. In fact the trial is littered with unsavory characters. But that's just my impression. Read for yourself and see what you conclude."

"I will, Dad. I can't thank you enough for your help." "It'll be thanks enough it we can just help that boy. I feel I know him before we even meet."

I lifted the cardboard box from his trunk with a groan. "I didn't know paper could be so heavy."

"I'll get the door." Dad rushed to hold the door wide. I struggled to maintain my grasp of the heavy container. My view of my feet was blocked so I shuffled slowly.

The tip of my shoe caught the door jam. With a muffled yelp I fell, still clutching the box. I landed sprawled on the pile of scattered computer printouts.

Before I could regain my footing, Beth rushed into the room.

"What was that noise?" Her gaze raked over my fallen body then on to my father. "Hello, Mr. Daniels."

"Beth, it's my fault," my dad volunteered. "I should have used two cartons."

"Two cartons? For what?" Beth directed her question to me as I pushed myself to a standing position. Better to face her on equal footing. I had wanted to explain Woody's court papers to Beth at an opportune time, which was not in the presence of my father.

With a deep breath, I said, "It's a trial transcript. Woody's." I waited and watched as Beth's face froze in anger. She didn't say a word. She didn't have to. Her actions spoke volumes as she spun on her heel and strode from the room.

"What's wrong with Beth?" my father asked, scratching his head.

"Oh, you know how women are. She doesn't understand why I want to get involved with a prisoner. She's afraid I'll let it interfere with my job. But I think this is a vital part of my work."

I stooped and gathered the papers and pitched them back into the cardboard box.

Dad dropped down and helped me gather the last remaining sheets.

"I hate to see this come between you and your wife."

"Dad, I just feel this is the right thing to do. Beth will come around when she realizes how seriously I take this responsibility, and that's what it is, a responsibility. It's a matter of justice." I picked up the heavy box and lugged it into the study and dropped it on the floor beside my desk. Dad laid the papers he carried on the pile. "This just fell on my shoulders and I'll continue in my efforts unless I get a sign from above to stop. I just hope that if the sign comes, I'll be able to recognize it."

My father breathed a long sigh. "Okay, whatever you decide, I'm behind you. Tell Beth goodbye for me."

"Yeah, Dad, I will. I'll call you after I schedule an appointment with Woody."

The day stretched out before me. I would have enough time to review the manuscript. I lifted the first official-looking page

The people of the state of Kentucky, plaintiff, vs. Woodrow Howard Pierce, defendant
Appearances:
For the people: office of the District Attorney
by Martin Brewster
Deputy District Attorney
for the defendant: law office of Jason Watts
112 N, Court Avenue, Graydon, Kentucky
witness index
For the People

I scanned the lengthy list of witnesses for the people; a dozen names. The names Dad had mentioned jumped out at me, all on the prosecution side; the bouncer at the club, the dancer, the fellow who owned the motel where Carrie was found. I made a mental note because my father thought them suspicious. But there were other names I wondered about, like a John Henson and Donald Mauk.

My mind reeled at the task of reviewing the court documents.

At the same time my heart picked up pace in excitement. It held incredible insight into the court system at work. I would be able to grasp every element of the case against Woody. I would hear what the jury heard. My hands shook.

The opening statements were lengthy as the deputy district attorney laid out his case.

He painted a picture of an angry young man prone to fits of violence, with a temper unchecked, a young man who indulged in heavy drink and deviant behavior. I skipped a few pages. The words: *Direct Examination by Martin Brewster* caught my eye.
Q: Deputy Rowe, can you state and spell your full name?
The Witness: Anthony Rowe, A-n-t-h-o-n-y R-o-w-e.
Q: How are you employed, sir?
A: I'm a deputy sheriff for the county Sheriff's Department.

I lightly scanned the witness's description of his background and training. Finally, the reason for his testimony became evident.

Q: On the date May 6, 2000, did you answer a call to the Starlite Motel in Jasper?

A: Yes sir. A Mr. Wade Adkins called and said he couldn't rouse a guest with her requested wake-up call at 8 o'clock. He went and knocked on her door.

When she didn't answer, he opened the door and found the victim dead in her bed. That's when he called our office.

Mr. McMann: Objection. The victim had not been pronounced dead by the coroner.

Court: Objection sustained.

Q: Deputy Rowe, would you describe the condition and circumstance of the victim when you entered the motel room.

A: Yes sir. She, the victim, was lying on the bed unclothed. Her hands were stretched above her head, like this, and tied to a section of the headboard. Her mouth had been stuffed with a wash cloth. Her, her throat had been cut, from ear to ear. The bed was soaked with her blood.

I dropped the paper. My hand trembled. I hadn't known Carrie had died so violently. Poor girl. What kind of monster had she crossed? A sickness gathered in my stomach as I visualized the scene. The girl had made so many bad choices in her young life, choosing to strip-dance to pay for college, getting involved with an underworld culture, exposing herself to the desires of any type of perverted male who paid the cover charge.

My dad always said you could never put an old head on young shoulders, meaning wisdom came only with age.

I picked up the paper again, driven to know it all, not only for Woody's sake but for Carrie's as well.

Mr. Brewster: I would, at this time, like to submit into evidence, this silk blood stained scarf.

Deputy, can you tell me where you found the scarf.

A: Yes, sir, that's what tied her hands to the headboard. We later learned the scarf was part of her dance outfit. She wore it around her chest, tied in a bow so it could be easily removed.

Mr. Watts: Objection to his last statement, hearsay.
Court: Sustained.
Q: Was the motel room disturbed in any way?
A: Oh yeah, beer bottles had been knocked over and the lamp and radio were lying on the floor like somebody had been in a rage.
Q: Had the door to the room been damaged? Was there any evidence to forced entry?
A: No sir, the door showed no signs of being forced.

I mused over that bit of information. The prosecution wanted the jury to believe that since there was no forced entry then Woody must be guilty. I believed it meant she knew the assailant and let him into her room. I would mentally make notes of the witnesses whom she might have known well enough to cause her to welcome one of them in.

The deputy had little else to offer the court, so I looked on in search of other information. Upon checking the notes I had made, I would skip to the testimony of other witnesses of interest, starting with the man who owned the motel, a Mr. Wade Adkins.

My gaze skimmed over the pages of text until I found his testimony.
Q: Would you state and spell your full name for the court?
A: Wade Adkins, W-a-d-e A-d-k-i-n-s.
Q: What is your occupation?
A: I own and operate the Starlite Motel in Jasper.
Q: Would you tell the court what happened on May 6, 2000.
A: Well sir, I gave Miss Lola
Mr.Watts: Objection. Would the witness please not refer to the victim by her stage name?
Court: Sustained. When speaking about the victim, please call her by Miss Simpson.
A: Well, as I was saying. I gave Miss Simpson a wakeup call at eight like she asked me to do. She always picks up, so when I got no answer, I got worried. I waited about fifteen minutes and rang again, still no answer, so I walked over to her room and knocked on her

door. I couldn't rouse her. Her car was parked in its usual place so I knew she was there.

Q: Go on, Mr. Adkins, what happened next?

A: Well, I peeked through the window but I couldn't see nothing. I hollered her name real loud and rapped on the pane. The place was as quiet as death itself.

MrWatts: Objection, please have the witness stick to the facts, your honor.

Court: So ordered. Mr. Adkins, the court doesn't need to hear your embellishments.

A: Yes, your honor. The place was quiet.

Q: What did you do next?

A: Well sir, I took my key and opened the door and I said, "Lola, time to get up." That's what I always called her. She didn't go by Carrie. Then I said, "Lola, are you okay?"

When she didn't answer, I flicked on the light. That's when I got sick and almost passed out. I hurried back to the office and called 911.Q: Mr. Adkins, did you hear any suspicious noise during the night? Did you hear any crying out in alarm or fright? Any screams for help?

A: No, sir. I manned the office until twelve then I closed up and retired. I run a small business. I only have ten rooms to let, so I take care of everything myself, except, of course, the housecleaning. I have two ladies who do that for me.

Q: Did you see the defendant, Woodrow Pierce, at any time during that night the victim was killed?

A: Yeah. He's a frequent visitor to Lola's; I mean Miss Simpson's room.

He came bounding through the parking lot in his big dually pickup truck.

 Thinks he's a big tough guy in his big tough truck.

Mr. Watts: Objection, your honor.

Court: Objection sustained. Mr. Adkins, I don't want to warn you again to stick to the facts of the case and keep your opinions to yourself.

Witness: Yes, your honor, I'm sorry.

Q: Did you ever see a show of temper from the defendant?

A: You bet. He's got a smart mouth. He's mad just about all the time.
He's cussed me out several times. He's mean through and through.

Mr. Watts: Objection, objection.

Mr. Brewster: I've no more questions of this witness, your honor.

Court: Mr. Watts, you may cross-examine this witness.

Mr. Watts: I have no questions of this witness at this time.

What? I couldn't believe what I was reading. I had questions. Who was this guy? What was his background? Where did he retire to on that fateful night? He seemed so resentful of Woody. Did he have a crush of Carrie? Was he married? A family man? He had a key to Carrie's room. He could have entered while she slept. Carrie didn't have to allow entry to the creep who killed her. Woody's attorney missed an opportunity to create doubt in the jury's minds. If the rest of the trial was handled as poorly as this witness's testimony, it was no wonder he was found guilty. I made notes of my thoughts. Woody had poor council at best.

Surely he would be granted a new trial if he had a new, more confident lawyer fighting for him.

I stretched for I had been sitting too long. A break was long overdue. Beth was out, probably shopping with Janice. She could spend hours wandering through the shops at the local mall, only to come home with a few meager purchases. I could never understand her passion. For me, shopping was done out of pure necessity. After a peanut butter and jelly sandwich and a glass of milk, I hurried back to my study.

Emotionally, had remained in that courtroom. I visualized each character, putting a face on every faceless figure. In my imagination, Mr. Wade Adkins was a thin man of about fifty years with thinning hair, poor posture and a hawkish nose. I shivered, not liking the man. Strange, how I could form such an opinion from such a brief examination. I often wondered if I had inherited my father's gift of insight.

Maybe his ability was acquired with age. I could only do my best and hope to grow in grace as he had done.

Whose testimony would I next scrutinize?

Miss Shapely Shaw intrigued me. Dad had mentioned her with an odd affection in his voice. After minutes of scanning text I finally found the entry.

Mr. Brewster: If it pleases the court, the people would like to call Miss Shapely Shaw to the stand.

The Clerk: Miss Shaw, Please raise your right hand. Do you solemnly swear that the testimony you are about to give in the case now pending before this court shall be the truth, the whole truth, and nothing but the truth, so help you, God?

The Witness: Yes, I swear.

The Clerk: Thank you. Please be seated.

Direct Examination

by Martin Brewster

Q: Will you spell and pronounce your full name for the court, please.

A: Okay, my name is S-h-a-p-e-l-y S-h-a-w, Shapely Shaw.

Q: Is that your legal name?

A: Yeah. I had it changed after I got my implants. I did it for my career you know.

Q: What do you do for a living?

A: I'm an exotic dancer. That's spelled X-otic with a big red X.

That was my idea, for my work at the Fantasy Nights club.

Q: Ma'am, were you acquainted with the victim in this case, Miss Carrie Ann Simpson?

A: Yeah, we were friends. Me and her both worked at the club. I was the first act of the evening. It was my job to warm up the guys; get them to loosen up and spend their money.

Carrie, she was the last act, kinda like the <u>grand finale.</u>

I started the action and she ended it.

Q: Are you also acquainted with the defendant, Woodrow Pierce?

A: Yes, he was at the club almost every weekend.

Q: What kind of man is Mr. Pierce, in your opinion?

A: Well, he's mean, when he has too much to drink, otherwise he's okay.

I slammed my fist against my desk repeatedly. Object, object. The attorney was leading his witness. Where was Woody's lawyer? He certainly was not on the job. I could have represented Woody better than his council. The man should be disbarred.

Q: Did you ever observe the defendant act in any violent way toward Carrie Simpson?

A: Oh yeah, he was very jealous. If Carrie got too close to a John, he'd grab her by the arm so tight she'd get bruised. And one time I saw him hit her, not that she didn't deserve it, but he slapped her so hard the imprint of his hand was left on her.

Defendant: She's lying. I never hurt Carrie, never.

Court: Council, will you refrain your client from such outbursts. This court does not allow this sort of disrespect.

Mr. Watts: Yes, your honor.

Mr. Brewster: No more questions of this witness, your honor. Your witness, Mr. Watts.

Cross Examination by Mr. Watts

Q: Miss Shaw, did you like Miss Simpson?

A: Yeah, we had a lot in common.

Q: Did you like Woodrow Pierce?

A: Yeah. All the girls called him pretty boy. He got his looks from his mother.

Q: The time you saw Mr.Pierce strike the victim, just where on her body did he slap her?

A: On her butt.

Q: Miss Shaw, did any of the men in the club ever slap you on your behind?

A: Oh yeah, lots of times. They're not supposed to touch us dancers but you know how rules are in a strip club.

Mr. Watts: No Miss Shaw, I'm afraid I don't know how it is in a strip club. Can you tell me?

A: Well, if a John has a bill in his hand, most girls will let them get close enough to tuck the bill inside their g-string. You see, we never get completely naked, just topless. So with a bill, a John can get a peek.

Q: Now I understand. So when the defendant smacked Carrie, had she gotten too close to a customer?

A: Yeah, real close.

The guy was flashing a hundred dollar bill and Carrie let him get real close?

Q: So, did the defendant express outrage? Was his temper unchecked? Did he grab Carrie and strike her with great force?

A: Oh no, he just smacked her and told her she was getting out of line. He said the bill wasn't worth the guy getting to feel her up.

Q: Miss Shaw, Carrie had very fair skin, didn't she? Skin that marred easily?

A: Yeah, she had beautiful skin. I guess you would call it ivory. And she had red hair. The Johns said she was milk and honey.

Q: So, the defendant wasn't pushed to violence, just to an expression of disapproval.

A: Yeah, I guess you could say that.

Q: Miss Shaw, do you think Woodrow Pierce is capable of killing Carrie Ann Simpson?

A: No.

Mr. Brewster: Objection, calls for a conclusion from the witness.

Court: Sustained.

Mr. Watts: No more questions of this witness, your honor.

I laid down the page of trial transcript. Miss Shaw's language disturbed me. I rubbed my hands down the cloth of my slacks as if to wipe away some contaminate. She had put Carrie in an unflattering situation.

Surely the girl's actions had not been so crude. If she had been willing to compromise herself in such a manner, what else might she have done? I had the sensation of stepping in quicksand, where I might be sucked in so deep; I would not be able to escape. Did I dare explore further. I could back out now and leave justice to the court. I rubbed my hand across my tired eyes. I didn't have to decide now. I could sleep on it. Maybe another day would bring a clearer view of my role.

I had to empty my brain of the farce of a trial. Woody had been doomed from the first drop of the gavel. This verdict couldn't stand, it just couldn't. I needed a couple of aspirins.

Chapter Seven

Sunday dawned with the sun streaming golden rays of warmth from a backdrop of milky blue sky. The temperature hovered at seventy degrees and would surely climb comfortably later in the day. "We should have a good turnout for the service today," I said to Beth at the breakfast table. Everything was right in my world on Sundays. It was my day to spread love. How many men could claim such an honor. I was truly blessed.

"Yes, the weatherman said the day would be beautiful."

"You're beautiful," I said. She wore a yellow dress with white dots, reminding me of sunshine. Her cheeks flushed and she lowered her gaze. My heart swelled. I hoped Beth never realized the power she held over me.

"What is today's sermon about?" she asked, attempting to deter my untimely attention.

I hesitated. A slight tinge of guilt dulled my happiness. "It's about dying. Since Janice so recently lost her father, I thought the subject might be appropriate."

"How thoughtful of you." Beth reached out her hand and covered mine.

I noted the softness of her touch. "I'm sure Janice will receive comfort from your words. You're so good at your job."

Now it was my turn to drop my head.

There wasn't enough time to write a sermon of any substance. I simply would have to go through with my plan of using the work of Reverend Roe. Silently, I vowed to myself, I would never again rely on another man's words. But for today, I would push away my misgivings.

I stood in my robe and gazed out over the congregation. The choir had sung and taken their seats behind me. The good weather had brought out every member and some guests. I went through the usual welcoming and announcements then the time came for my sermon. I took a deep breath and in Roe's eloquent words spoke of the incredible beauty of life and the uncertainty of the future.

"My dear friends, life is a journey of hills and valleys. The highs are filled with light and warmth and love and happiness. But there are valleys in our journey, valleys filled with dark shadows and cool wind. Did you ever notice that within fertile valleys is where the sweetest most abundant fruit grows?

If your life was spent on that warm bright hilltop, you could not grow spiritually. Trials in life are what gives us strength."

My gaze fell to Janice.

Surely she would find comfort with Reverend Roe's words. A frown creased her face as if she were disturbed.

I continued. "You see, the fruit is the bad times of your life.

Your losses and your pain are what make you grow. After several gloomy days we are so grateful to see the sun, but with many days of sunshine you lose that appreciation. We might even say, sure is hot today, we could use a little relief. Pain adds a desired element to the human nature. So take comfort from your pain, feel it, mourn your loss and grow in grace. When you know pain, you will be more sensitive to others who are suffering because you have been there; you will love life more."

I glanced to Janice again. She appeared angry, even hostile. Maybe she was inconsolable and would just have to work through her grief in her own way. I turned my attention to the others in the congregation and continued Roe's sermon.

After the service, Beth and I stood at the doorway to acknowledge each one attending. Normally, I would receive numerous compliments on my sermon, but today, there were few. Uneasiness gnawed at me stomach. Janice stepped stiffly as she exited. She turned toward me.

I extended my hand but she didn't respond, instead, she lowered her voice and with vehemence said, "I know what you did. That sermon was Reverend Roe's. He composed it especially for me when my mother died.

I have a copy of it in my Bible. Just wait until the board hears about this."

At my side, Beth gasped, and then she whimpered like a puppy and pulled her hand from mine. The minutes passed slowly until we had shaken hands with the last person exiting the church. As soon as decorum allowed, Beth whirled and sped toward the parsonage.

I followed her with labored steps.

A weight lay heavily on my shoulders. I had gotten caught the one and only time I had ever cheated in my life. Beth must feel so disappointed in me. The indiscretion hadn't seemed of much importance to me but it was evidently going to be of relevance to others.

Beth turned her anger on me as soon as I closed the door behind me. "How could you, Harley? How could you have done such a thing? You never had a problem with words before. Why now?" She threw her purse on the sofa.

"I . . . I ran out of time and felt pressured, and Roe wrote such beautiful sermons. I thought . . . just once." How could I explain my actions to Beth when I didn't understand myself.

"What pressures did you have that you didn't always have?" Beth stood with her head lowered. Her red hair gleamed.

Anger contorted her features. I was reminded of a bull just before he charged.

"On Friday, the youth group meeting took longer than usual and you wanted to go to dinner." I ran out of words.

"What? Don't blame this on me. We could have eaten later or I could have called Janice, anything but what you did. There was

Saturday. You had all day. Why couldn't you have written on Saturday?" Beth waited for my answer, restlessly tapping her foot.

I hedged her question. "I wanted to comfort Janice and just couldn't find the proper words. I can't relate to her. Reverend Roe had written perfectly what I couldn't express."

"Harley, I know you don't particularly care for Janice but she and I are becoming good friends."

"It's not that I don't like her, I couldn't write for her, couldn't find the motivation. I guess I should have just gone on to another subject instead." I rubbed my hand over my face. If only I could wipe away the anguish I felt inside. I was afraid I had gotten myself into real trouble with the church.

"You could have quoted Reverend Roe. They would have understood if you would have told them you were using his words."

"You're right, you're right. I just didn't think."

"You know you have to address them at the evening service. What will you say? Please think of something to smooth this thing over."

My mind spun.

Usually the twilight service consisted of song and prayer with only a short address by me. "I'll thank Reverend Roe for the inspiration for this morning's sermon. It will be a little late but maybe they won't be so bothered by my omission this morning." Small beads of perspiration popped out on my forehead. I wiped them away with my handkerchief.

"I hope not. I'll apologize to Janice. Don't you ever do anything so stupid ever again." Beth gripped her hands into fists.

"I just don't understand you. God gave you the gift of wonderful speech. You didn't have to do this, Harley"

I stood helpless against her rage. I had no defense. I stepped over to the wide window of the living room and gazed out at our beautiful church and grounds. A few parishioners stood yet in small circles, talking, their heads together, as if whispering secretively.

They seemed to be throwing angry glances toward the parsonage. Surely my imagination was growing too active. I wiped my hands over my eyes. Janice stepped apart and stared toward where I stood at the window.

"Lunch is ready. I prepared a stew earlier in the crock pot." Beth's voice was cool, not in the least inviting. I would try to eat but an odd lump had formed in my throat. Swallowing would be difficult.

Maybe a glass of lemonade would help clear my throat.

I poured myself a tall glass of the cool tart liquid. Yes, I received some relief but I knew my food would be tasteless.

I would eat but only for sustenance. That evening I retired to my study. A tension lay between Beth and me. There had been little reaction from the congregation when I made my reference to the former reverend and his inspiration. My imagination had probably blown the whole situation out of proportion. I had learned a hard lesson. Never again would I put myself in such a compromising situation. The phone rang and I picked up the receiver. "Hello."

"Hello, Son."

"Oh, hi Dad."

"Well, did you set up the appointment?"

"Appointment?" Quickly I searched my mind.

"At the prison, to see Woody. I'm really anxious to meet that boy. In fact I can't get him out of my mind."

I had forgotten. I was supposed to call Dad and let him know. "Yes, Dad, tomorrow morning, at ten, in the meeting hall. I meant to call you."

I was losing some of my enthusiasm for this venture. My every attempt brought consequences.

Maybe I was moving in a direction I wasn't supposed to go. Perhaps I should forget about Woody, innocent or not, and just stick to my preaching.

"I'll come by your place about nine."

"All right, Dad. I'll be ready. See you then."

The ball had been set in motion. I might as well let it roll and see where it went. One more visit with Woody couldn't hurt. In fact I felt a need to see him one more time.

Chapter Eight

The massive structure was as imposing as ever. Dad and I sat for a moment in the parking lot that faced Eddyville prison before exiting his Buick. "Man, what a place," he said. "I don't think I've ever been this close to 'the castle'; gives me the chills. I've heard it's hard time in there."

"It's maximum prison, Dad." I breathed a long breath, almost of dread. Where was life taking me? Was it only three months ago Beth and I moved to Landon? We both had been so excited to settle in a new town and meet new people. The farthest thing from my mind had been a prison called Eddyville and a prisoner whom I would come to believe depended on me to come to his aid, save his life. I was yet uncomfortable in this role as savior, not sure if the task was God's will or just my own.

I slowed my climb up the concrete steps so Dad could keep up. We entered through the heavy metal door, and then passed through a metal detector.

"What do we do now?"

Dad glanced around, taking in the high ceiling of the old structure.

"This place looks ancient but impressive. Builders don't do work like this anymore."

"The other buildings are newer. Come with me.

We'll go to the administration office and get a pass then a guard will escort us to the meeting hall.

Woody will sit with us at a small table. You will be close and personal.

We sat down in our appointed chairs. Guards stood behind glass barriers at either side of the room. I felt strange. Would Woody be as I remembered? Would he even remember me? We watched as he entered the room from the opposite side. For a moment he looked unsure. I noticed he had gotten thinner. Maybe Mom could send him some of her chocolate chip cookies.

He noticed us. His face broke into a wide smile as he shuffled over to take his seat just opposite us. "Hello, Woody, " I said.

"Hi, Preacher, how's it going?"

"Well, some interesting things have been happening. I'd like you to meet my father, Boyd Daniels."

"Hello, Sir."

Woody eyed my dad, sizing him up. A reserve literally pulled his body back until he sat stiff and unyielding. Dad in turn, leaned forward, his gaze probing the prisoner.

"Hello, Woody.

My son has told me a lot about you and your case. He and I want to help you if we can."

"Why would you want to help me? You don't even know me." His eyes darkened.

"I read your trial transcript.

I'm acquainted with the circumstances surrounding your conviction. I think there's cause for a new trial. I don't think you had proper council."

"Yeah, the guy who was my lawyer thought I was guilty. He didn't like me either which was a big problem."

"It was more than a problem, it was disaster," my father said.

"The guy was all wrapped up in his own problems. His wife was stepping out on him. He was crazy with jealousy. That's all he talked about. His mind was elsewhere during the trial. He treated me like I was the other guy. I never fooled around with married women, I swear."

63

"Well, that's one avenue we can pursue but the most important one is who really did the crime. You knew Carrie and you knew the people where she worked. Do you have any idea as to who could have killed her?"

"I don't know, Mr. Daniels. I've gone over everyone in my mind. You'd think anyone that demented would stand out in a crowd but I can't think of anyone who looked like a murderer." Woody's face creased into a troubled mask.

Dad was persistent with his questions. His gaze burned into Woody's eyes. "Who may have been jealous? Evidently Carrie was beautiful. She's sure to have had men infatuated with her."

"Yeah, just about everybody she met. Old or young, they all fell at her feet." Woody's eyes shone with pride as he spoke about the girl he obviously adored. "She wasn't just pretty, she was smart and friendly. She liked everybody, said each was beautiful in his own way. I know that got her in trouble. She was too trusting, gave everyone the benefit of doubt. Her world was a great place. . . until some son of a . . . . turned on her."

"Did she mention to you about being afraid of anyone?

Sometimes women have good instincts about things like that. Maybe someone following her? Think hard. There have to be incidents of importance somewhere in your memory." Dad surprised me with his interrogation of Woody. All the while he intently studied the young man's face.

Woody closed his eyes and rubbed his fingers across his forehead. "There was a customer who was always flashing big bills at Carrie, thought he could buy her.

He always wanted to take her (away from all this). He could have the other girls, but even he saw Carrie was special."   ↵

"Do you know his name?"

I pulled out my notepad to jot down the name.

"Yes, of course, that's easy. His name was Juan Manos. Carrie nicknamed him Don Juan. She actually liked him. He watched after her. He acted like he owned the place and everyone in it." My mind seized the information. I recalled the dancer's testimony at the trial. She would recognize the guy with the big bills, the one who touched Carrie.

"Anyone else?" Dad prodded him.

"Oh yeah, there's Alfred Dugall. He dates Carrie's mom. But in my opinion he was more interested in Carrie. I could see it in his eyes, you know?"

"Yes, we know," Dad agreed. "The eyes tell you everything."

"Except when it comes to the big stuff, like murder," Woody said, his voice sounding hopeless. His thin shoulders slumped beneath the red jumpsuit he wore.

"Maybe we just have to look into the right eyes. Guilt has a way of weighing on a person. With enough pressure even the most hardened can crack," Dad replied.

Hope sprang in Woody's eyes.

"Do you really think there's hope? Are you really going to follow through with this?"

"Yes, oh yes we are. With a little help from God," I said.

"Oh, God" Woody's voice fell. "Can't we just leave him out of this? He's never been on my side before, why should I think he'll help me now?"

"He brought me to you," I said. "If I hadn't been his servant, we never would have met."

"Well, I'm not holding my breath till he comes to my aid."

Dad spoke with a tenderness in his voice.

"Don't give up, Son. We're going to see this through, you'll see."

"I'd like to have hope, Sir. But this place kind of drains it from me. Man, I'd like to go home . . . just for awhile." Woody held his head in his hands with his face hidden. A sound burst from him, almost a sob, but with a quick jerk he steeled himself. He was used to doing that, I could tell.

"Sorry, I was just thinking about home.

The tobacco crops should be ripening about now. Strange how memories will hang in your mind. With me, it's the smell of a field of tobacco. I was a farm hand when I was a kid, made pretty good spending money.

Did you ever grow tobacco?" His gaze questioned me then my father.

"No, I know nothing about the crop," I said and Dad shook his head in agreement.

"Well, when the plants get yea tall," Woody held out his hand to indicate the height, we had to top them.

The plants would spread and the leaves widen. When I'd walk through the rows I'd get covered with sticky gum from the plants.

I would go home and Mom would meet me at the door with a towel and a bar of soap. 'You smell to high Heaven, she'd say.' "

He gave a horse chuckle."I'd liked to have farmed for a living but unless you own the land you can't make it, and even then it's a meager existence."

Woody caught himself and apologized. "I'm sorry, I got carried away."

"I don't blame you for being homesick," I said. "That's beautiful country."

"I don't think I could make it here if I believed I would never go home again. I think I would die before they had to kill me. I guess I'm hoping for that miracle."

"Well, you're going home again; you're not going to die here. Don't you forget that, Son." My dad's voice was thick with emotion. I noted the endearment he had used toward Woody. Dad would move Heaven and Earth for his kids.

In a way he had just adopted Woody. Relief flooded through me. Woody's eyes brightened. Somehow Dad and I would free this young man from prison and he would go home again.

I knew this with a certainty, I just didn't know how . . . yet.

After an hour-long visit, Dad and I left the prison. We were both lost in thought as we began the drive home. Quietness grew between us.

Finally, Dad spoke, "My heart is beating faster just at the thought of where we might be headed. What a ride this is going to be."

"What does Mom say about your involvement in this?"

"Oh, you know your mother, she's content with her garden club and friends, and leaves me to my own devices. I mentioned Woody and my visit with him today. She just said, 'All right Dear'." Dad chuckled.

I laughed too but didn't reply. In my mind, I thought, *I wish Beth was that understanding.*

Chapter Nine

Dad didn't take time to come inside when we got back to my place. Instead, he dropped me off to continue his journey on home. "I'll be in touch, Harley, as soon as I have anything of interest to report to you."

"Thanks, Dad." What a guy. My heart swelled. I stood in the yard to stretch my legs. I was caught by the beauty of the sunset. The church and parsonage sat on a rise where we had a clear view of the setting sun. In fact, our first sight of the place in which we now resided had been in the evening. The scene was bathed in bright hues, like a Monet painting. The parsonage was of a quaint English cottage style with an arched doorway and a matching arched gate leading to the garden.

The church was a modest structure by some standards with the usual white pillars and stained glass windows. The steeple was of greatest interest.

Added at a later date, the decorative spire was a little more ornate with a copper roof and copper colored bell.

Beth really liked living here.

I drew a deep breath. For some reason I was hesitating about entering the dwelling. A strange sense of foreboding overtook me. Something wasn't right. My steps slowed as I strode up the path and opened the walnut stained door. Beth was pacing the expanse of the living room. She turned at my entrance. Her face was red and streaked from crying.

"What's wrong?" My heart tore in my chest. I rushed to take my wife in my arms but she pushed me away.

"The church board has called a special meeting tomorrow morning at nine." Her words were caught between sniffs as she tried to curb her emotions.

"A meeting? About what?"

"I'm not sure but I didn't like the tone of Janice's voice. She was cool and . . .and. I thought we were friends."

Beth put a tissue to her nose and blew. "I'm sure it won't be good news. I don't think they like us, Harley."

"Beth, you're letting your imagination run away with you. It could be something as simple as finances. You know we've asked for a plumber. There are so many leaks around here."

"No, I could tell. It's more serious than that." She groaned. "We're going to get turned out of the church. I can just feel it."

"But we haven't had a chance. We've only been here a few months. Surely these people are more understanding than that."

"It's you, Harley."

Beth turned the full force of her anger on me. "You haven't been giving your best. You've been preoccupied. Don't think Janice hasn't noticed."

"I'll admit I've made a couple of mistakes, but it won't happen again."

"Yes it will, as long as you're involved with that prisoner. That's where you were today, wasn't it? Tell me the truth. I want to know."

I hadn't told Beth of my visit to the prison. To do so would have just stirred her anger. I had stated I was spending some time with my father, which was true.

"Well, weren't you?"

"Yes, Dad and I visited Woody."

"Oh, there will never be an end to this." Beth stormed from the room. I dropped down on the sofa. Hopelessness engulfed me. Things were getting out of control. I would give up my endeavor. I had no choice. My job and even my marriage were at stake. I couldn't jeopardize the things that meant most in my life.

That was just too high a cost. Woody's young face flashed in my mind and I felt tightness in my throat. I pushed his image away.

The thought of the night spent with Beth's rigid body scooted to the farthest reaches of her side of the bed taunted me. I wouldn't join her. Instead, I stretched out on the sofa. I didn't expect much sleep anyway, not with tomorrow's meeting looming over me.

I closed my eyes and in spite of the circumstance, fell immediately into dreamless slumber.

Wakefulness came slowly with the dawn. I found my body sprawled with one leg hanging off the edge of the sofa. I felt stiff and sore but my mind had rested. I stumbled into the kitchen to brew a pot of coffee. After a steaming cup and the brightness of morn, my mood lifted. Surely Beth had over-reacted. We would meet with the board members and settle whatever trivial matter was at hand.

Beth spoke in a quiet manner at breakfast. She kept her cool gaze downcast.

But at least she spoke, I told myself. We both kept glancing at the clock. Nine o'clock arrived all too soon.

Beth and I walked silently out the front doorway and down the brick path to the pastor's office where all the church business was handled. The entire board was seated around the walnut table, all twelve members. The secretary had a pen and pad lying in front of her. My gaze quickly scanned each unreadable face.

"Good morning, everyone," I said.

"Good morning," they responded in unison.

"What's going on? Is anything wrong?"

My heart began to pick up pace. Janice cleared her throat. "Yes, Reverend. Something is wrong.

We have voted. We think you're wrong . . .uh . . . wrong for our church."

Beth gasped and dropped into a chair. I stood frozen.

"How could you make that determination so soon? I've only been your minister a few months. We've just gotten settled in. We're still in a period of adjustment, not only me but the church body too." Disappointment and anger surged inside me. Did they want me to beg? Would it do any good?

"Why? I think you owe me an explanation." I dared to challenge the woman who sat at the head of the table, Beth's so-called friend.

"You don't seem to have concern for the members of this church.

Do you really want me to list the grievances against you?" Her face was unsmiling as her eyes clashed with mine. "It is of great length."

"Yes, what have I done that is so terrible as to warrant a dismissal from my position?"

My voice was strained and I could feel the blood rush to my face.

Beth reached up and grabbed my sleeve. "No, Harley, let it go. They have the right. We knew that."

"Well, Miss Holland?" I stood my ground.

I had the right to know. A few members squirmed in their chairs. Janice cleared her throat.

"Well, Reverend, if you insist. You simply have not fulfilled your duties like hospital visits."

"Only once; I forgot." I replied."Otherwise I have faithfully made my rounds."

Janice's face hardened. Her gaze raked rudely over me.

"What is your excuse for Sunday's sermon? I know you didn't write it because Reverend Roe wrote it especially for me when I lost my mother. I have a copy in my Bible. I knew the speech by heart.

He touched me so deeply with his words, his words, Reverend Daniels," she repeated.

The woman's voice grew more strident.

"You can't deny that you stole his work and passed it off as your own, a deed I feel is unscrupulous at best."

Beth drew a quick intake of breath. "I . . I did not steal. Inspiration . . . would not come." I sputtered and turned my back to the group. What could I say? Surely what I had done was not thievery. I had done wrong, yes, but . . . My thoughts faltered.

"We are kind people," Janice said, in her smug voice that tormented me. I suddenly knew the meaning of the old adage *rubbing salt in a wound.* Her voice actually brought pain to my chest. "We've decided to give you a two month sabbatical to find another position. Of course, you'll continue to receive your pay.

As of today, you are relieved of your position here at the Trinity Way Church."

Just like that, it was over. I had no recourse. I had been fired. My service, which I loved, was not wanted, not here. I turned and stumbled from the church. Beth followed. I was numbed by what had just happened.

I was a preacher with no congregation.

I could not stand in the pulpit and tell of my Lord. Moisture welled in my eyes but I quickly wiped it away.

Once inside the parsonage, I dropped to the sofa. Beth had been quiet but when she closed the door behind her, she lashed out at me. "I knew it. I knew we were in trouble. It's entirely your fault, Harley, you and your crusade. If you hadn't been so absorbed by your obsession of saving a murderer, this wouldn't have happened.

I knew this was too good to last. What are you going to do, Harley?"

I glanced up, my gaze meeting her furious eyes.

"I don't know.

Surely I'll be able to find another position. I'll contact the seminary. They're great at placements.

"When?"

"I don't know, but soon. I have two months."

Beth turned and swept the living room with her gaze. "I just painted. We haven't even unpacked everything." Her voice held an element of desperation. "Where will we live?"

"We could move into my parent's house. The basement is a separate apartment, you know. Each of us kids took a turn there as we broke away. It's already furnished and has a separate private entrance."

"No. I can't believe you would even suggest such a thing.

Move in with your mother and father? I won't do that. Harley."

"Beth, we have some savings, a few thousand but that wouldn't last long with the expense of a new place."

She paced the floor in front of me. "Well, you can go live with your parents. I want to go home to my Mom."

"Beth, you don't mean that."

My voice was horse and breathless. An agonizing feeling hit me in waves. "Please don't leave me."

"You should have considered that while you were shirking your duties."

"Beth, I'm human. I made some mistakes."

"Yes, and now you have to pay the consequences. I just need some time away from you. I want some space and time to think."

"All right, if you're sure that's what you want, I won't stop you. Will you keep in touch?"

"Yes, I'll call you. Keep the cell phone. I'll use Mom's."

"I love you, Beth."

"Don't try to change my mind, Harley."

"I wasn't trying to change your mind. I know better." I did love her even when she raged at me. My feelings for her had never wavered and they never would. Love for her consumed my heart.

"I'm going for a walk." She grabbed a sweater from the hall closet. A chill had hung in the morning air even though the sun shone brightly.

I didn't reply, just watched as she strode out the front door. The house grew silent. I felt stunned. My mind refused to cope with the events of the last hour.

How could this have happened? In a short span of time my whole world had crumbled and lay in shattered pieces at my feet. The phone rang and I jumped. My nerves were on edge too. I didn't want to answer, but after five insistent rings, I dragged myself from the couch and stumbled into the kitchen where the phone hung on the wall.

"Hello," I said in a deadened voice.

"Reverend?"

"Yes."

"This is Howard James. Remember me?"

My bruised mind tried to recall. The name was familiar.

"You and I talked. I'm the friend of Summer Pierce."

"Oh yes, Howard. I remember you well. How are you?" I tried desperately to regain some sense of normalcy.

"I'm good. The reason I called is the guy who was seeing Carrie Ann's mother. Well, he beat her up. He's in jail. I told you he was a bad egg. I'll bet he was the one who killed the poor girl."

"I don't think I'm going to continue with Woody's case, Howard. I'm in over my head. There have been too many repercussions."

The man was silent for a moment. "Want to tell me about it?"

I felt I owed him an explanation.

"I was getting too involved. I lost my position . . my job. I've been turned out of my church." I had to pause for my voice broke. I swallowed.

" And on top of that my wife is leaving me."

My words were just too heavy, sounding like a line from a bad movie. I laughed at the absurdity of them. "So, how was your day?"

He laughed in return."Sounds like you need a drink."

"I'll settle for a friendly shoulder."

"You got that. What are you going to do?"

"I don't know. I guess for now, I'll move back with my parents."

"Do you really want to do that?"

"No, that's the last thing I want to do." I admitted to him and myself.

"Well, I could offer you an alternative. I have two apartments over my garage. I live in one, the other is empty.

You're more than welcome to stay here as long as you need."

I hesitated. This turn of events was staggering, but timely.

"It's furnished. All you need is a few towels, sheets and things like that."

I had to think before I replied. Go to eastern Kentucky to live? Could I do such a thing?

"You'll be close to where the crime happened. You could better investigate the case. I'll help."

Still I hesitated. "I'm not sure, Howard."

"You know, I'm not a strong spiritual man but it seems (in my life anyway) that when God closes a door, he also opens a window. I don't believe anything happens by chance. There's a purpose in everything."

Suddenly, my heart grew light. Everything was fine. Howard was much more spiritual than he realized. He had just given me a gift, a blessing. Moments before he called I had asked the Lord for guidance. The window had been opened. I would take my cue. "Thanks, Howard. I will move into the apartment."

"Great. When?"

"Tonight. I'll immediately pack my things. I should be there by dusk."

"I'll be watching for you. See you then."

"Yes, and thanks again."

I whistled Amazing Grace as I pulled my luggage from the closet. If I'd had a voice, I would have sung. Before long, I was packed.

As I zipped my last bag, the front door slammed. Beth was back.

A look of surprise replaced the scowl on her face when she saw what I was doing. "Where are you going?" She had placed emphasis on the word you and I realized I had beaten her at her game.

She was the one who should pack and storm from the house to leave me upset and dejected, alone in my misery. I couldn't help but smile.

"I've been invited to spend a few days with a friend and I've accepted the invitation." I picked up my cases. "Enjoy your time with your mother." I stepped close and gave her a kiss on the cheek.

"Call me if you need anything." I resumed my whistling as I left the house. I hesitated about taking the better vehicle and leaving Beth the old van but she hadn't far to go and I would be back in rugged terrain. I would be better off in the new SUV.

In a few hours I would be back in hill country. With a long sigh, I pulled out onto the road and headed east toward the rising sun.

Chapter Ten

The road stretched before me, winding and familiar. I didn't have to check the map. I knew the way. As last time, I slowed my vehicle for the last miles. With my side window open I drew deeper breaths, inhaling the essence of the hills. I turned my radio on and searched for a station with a strong signal. Regional University Public Radio broadcasts boomed clear. Musicians strummed stringed instruments, producing the happiest sounds I had ever heard and voices sang in great vocal harmonies. Traditional old-time mountain music, the emcee called it. How could I have lived twenty-eight years and never have heard the music of my ancestors. My fingers tapped in rhythm to *Sally Goodin* and *Ain't Guine Drink A No More.*

I had found something else to love about eastern Kentucky. If I could find a source, I would purchase this music.

I reached my destination in late afternoon. Howard's garage was a hub of activity. All four bays were filled, with vehicles waiting. The clank of metal, the hiss of air hoses and laughing male voices combined in a den of healthy noise. I braked and turned off my engine. A familiar figure broke away from the others and strode toward me with a big smile on his face.

"Hi, Preacher, it's good to see you again." He wiped his hands on a grease streaked towel and thrust one hand forward.

"Hello, Howard." I reached out and we shook hands. "I'd like to thank you again for the invitation."

"My pleasure. Just doing my part. Kind of nice to feel like a part of divine intervention." He grinned and relief flooded through me. I had done the right thing in coming east. "Pull around behind the garage. There's a stairway. The first door on the right is where you'll be staying." He reached into his pocket and pulled out a key and handed it to me. "Make yourself at home. Do you have any plans for supper?"

"No, I've no plans," I said with a laugh.

"Well, come along with Summer and me. We're going to a wiener roast and hay ride. I told her you were coming for a visit, so she won't be surprised to see you.

"Thank you, but I hate to intrude."

"No intrusion, I swear. The event is sponsored by our local community church. Everybody's welcome. The food won't be fancy, just hotdogs and chips, maybe some beans, stuff like that." I hesitated.

"Come on, it'll be great," he urged.

"All right, you've convinced me."

I glanced down at my neatly creased navy slacks and my white shirt and realized I wasn't dressed for the occasion. I had never had much need for casual attire, duty was always calling.

Howard seemed to read my mind. "There's a thrift store just down the road. You can pick up some duds there."

"Duds?"

"Yeah, old clothes.

I'd hate to see you get your Sunday best suit all messed up."

"Well, I guess I'd better get settled in," I said as I fingered the brass key.

"Yeah, I'll be getting through here about five. As soon as I can get ready, we should leave for the roast. I'll see you later."

The apartment was quite nice, clean and functional. A bag of coffee lay on the counter next to the coffeemaker. In the refrigerator were basics like milk, juice and eggs. Prepared dinners were stored in the freezer. Howard and Summer were more than kind. I had to repay them. With only two months to aid Woody, I had to form a plan.

Upon entering the bedroom, I found the bed dressed in crisp white cotton sheets and the cover turned down in welcome. Good, for I had forgotten to bring linens. I had left home in a hurry, needing to put distance between myself and the parish and Beth. I stared at the bed. Tonight would be the first night I had slept alone since mine and Beth's wedding night. I sat down on the edge of the bed and dropped my head.

"God," I prayed, "help me to be strong, and do your bidding."

My life had taken such a strange turn. In a wave I was struck by the circumstance in which I found myself. A sense of unreal hit me. I had never been one to venture out of the norm, had never sought adventure, was content in the structure of routine yet here I was in a strange part of the state with strangers yet felt I belonged here.. My life was out of control except for the sense of purpose that was beginning to consume me.

I hung my slacks and shirts in the closet.

Howard would be getting off work in a couple of hours. I would have time to visit the thrift store if I hurried. I grabbed my keys. Within minutes I was staring at the store front of *Yours and Mine*, the only business on a street of rundown vacant buildings. Paint was peeling from the window frames and the doorknob hung loosely on the door. I entered to an overwhelming attic odor. Shelves lined the walls, all stacked with assorted items of clothing. Through the center of the room was an unkempt group of chairs and tables and lamps and assorted items of questionable taste.

"Hello, stranger." A large older lady in a print dress sat in one of the stuffed chairs. She placed her hands on either arm of the chair and pushed her heavy body upward. She waddled toward me on legs swollen with protruding purplish veins.

"How did you know I was a stranger?"

"Honey, I know every young face in this whole county, especially if they are handsome and yours ain't one of them. What can I do for you?"

"I would like to buy a couple pair of jeans and shirts. I've been invited to a hay ride and I don't have anything to wear."

"Oh yeah, that bunch of do-gooders at the church up the road is having it. They've always got some kind of nonsense going on.

Let me see." She looked me up and down. "I guess you to be a 32 waist and a 32 inseam and a medium shirt." She smiled. "How'd I do?"

"You did fine. That's my size exactly."

She pushed frizzy brown and red hair with gray roots off her forehead.

"I been doing this for a long time. It's an exact science. You want Levis?"

"Yes, Levis would be great if you have them." I rubbed my hands down my blended slacks.

"Everybody wants them so my supply might be low. Most everybody around here is a 36 or a 38." Her voice trailed off as she waddled toward the rear of the store.

"You're in luck," she called from the back of the room.

Next, she made her way to a rack and thumbed through some hanging garments. She mumbled something and glanced at me as if deciding which pattern would best suit me. Finally, she came forward and thrust the clothes out toward me. "These are about the best I can do."

The jeans were quite good, barely worn. The shirts were khaki colored knits, not what I would have chosen for myself, but under the circumstance I wasn't about to object.

"I always wash all the clothes I get before I stock them," the lady said.

I couldn't help but doubt her words. "How much?" I asked.

"The pants are three dollars each and the shirts are two dollars each. That'll be ten."

"Wow, that's a very good price," I said as I paid her.

"Well, all this stuff is donated. Most of it comes out of the northern states, some kind of Appalachian Aid Association. They think we poor hill people are in dire need. Ought to take care of their own, I say. Did you ever see the slums in those big cities and the homeless people?" She didn't wait for a reply to her question.

"I see them on TV, but no, they pretend not to see those poor folk.

Instead, they send stuff to us lesser creatures of the hills." She chuckled. "But that's okay."

The lady dropped back into her chair and put the money in a tin box lying on the table. "If they really wanted to help us, they'd bring back the jobs. This area made clothes, just like you're holding, in garment factories. They didn't pay great wages, but decent, a family could get by if they were careful, especially with a garden and a paying crop. Most people depended on a tobacco check at the end of the year. First they take the jobs away and give them to Mexico. Next, the government is going to do away with tobacco. It's no wonder the young people are getting into dope. They're without hope, can't afford college (and we have some nice universities nearby) and they've got no means to make a decent living."

"I didn't realize the economy was so devastated here."

"Neither does the government."

"Are illegal drugs a big problem as well?"

"Yeah. People are looking for an escape, I think, especially the young ones.

Drugs offer that, if only temporarily, then before they know it, they're hooked, which leads to crime because they don't have the money to buy more drugs.

It's a shame about that Pierce boy. Do you know him?" She paused and peered at me.

I was surprised at her sudden shift in conversation. She had mentioned Woody. I hesitated. "Yes . . . yes I know him."

"That boy didn't do that crime.

I knowed him since he was knee high to a grasshopper.

Somewhere in the mix, drugs were involved, you mark my words," she said wisely.

The slam of the door halted our conversation. A young man entered carrying a cardboard box filled with objects of glass and ceramic figurines. My eyes met his and he glanced quickly away. The proprietor picked up the tin that held her funds and slipped it into her pocket.

"Ma'am, would you be interested in buying these things. You see, I just lost my job and I need to buy some groceries." The youth shifted nervously from one foot to the other. His figure was gaunt, much too thin for a healthy young male.

The woman heaved a long sigh. "Let me see what you have here." He placed the box on a table for her to inspect the contents. He paced the floor while she lifted and checked the items. I wondered, maybe the things were stolen. The boy was much too nervous.

"Twenty is about all I can do, Son," she said, with a sad shake of her head.

"Twenty's fine," the young man replied and stuck out his hand.

She turned her back to him and fumbled in her pocket for the bill. When she turned he grabbed the money from her. "Thanks," he said in a dead voice then rushed to exit the store.

She looked at me, "See what I mean?"

At my quizzical stare, she said. "That poor young man is hooked. Couldn't you tell?"

I had no idea, how could I have? I had never before seen a person who used drugs. "Are you sure?"

"Oh, yes.

Did you see how he couldn't stand still? He needed a fix real bad." She looked into the box she had just purchased. "Now, what am I going to do with this stuff?

Poor kid, twenty dollars won't last him no time."

I glanced at my watch. Time was slipping away. "Thank you." I said as I picked up my package.

"Anytime, come back and see me again."

"If I need more clothes, I will." I left the shop. The apartment was equipped with a washer and dryer. I would stop at the small convenience store I had passed and purchase a box of detergent. There should be time for a wash and dry cycle.

By five o'clock I was dressed in my clean, new, used casual clothes. The garments fit perfectly. I hadn't worn jeans since I was a teenager and had forgotten how good they felt. Maybe tomorrow I could splurge and purchase a new pair of walking shoes. Somehow my black oxfords didn't blend with my new attire.

Soon I heard Howard bound up the stairs to his apartment. He was whistling as he ascended.

How long had it been since I had felt like whistling?

I couldn't remember. Then I chided myself, I had never been one to whistle. I sat down to wait for Howard's knock at the door. My journal lay beside me so I picked it up and made notes of my experiences today- the drive, my visit to the thrift store.

I recalled the words of the old character who tended the business. Could drugs have really played a part in Woody's case? No one had even mentioned the possibility. The seed the woman planted took root and grew.

This opened up a whole new avenue of exploration and a new, wider list of suspects and motives.

My heart picked up pace. Why should I be surprised at the prospect, I wasn't that uninformed.

I could easily get in over my head if I plunged blindly into this mess. Caution would have to rule my actions.

I had heard about what happened to people who tried to infiltrate the drug traffic in this part of the state.

One particular story had made the newspaper in Owensboro. Two undercover agents had been found face down in a creek bed. Their hands had been tied behind their backs and they each had taken a bullet to the head. Their cover- two guys joy riding on their four-wheelers. The man who owned the property on which they were trespassing fled the state. When the police closed in on him, they found he had committed suicide, or so the note he left stated. I had not doubted the elements of the story I had read at the time.

But now, I thought, how convenient that the guilty party would kill himself. The whole matter would be closed - the drug investigation and the murders. Some poor soul had taken the blame and had then been silenced.

I jumped and ducked my head. A knock at the door had cracked through the still room like the shot of a pistol and I had ducked as if a real bullet had been fired. I closed my journal, realizing I had gotten too carried away.

Howard stood in the doorway, his hair still wet from his shower.

"Are you ready to go?" he asked. He peered at me closely. "You okay?"

"Yes, I'm fine," I assured him. "I'm starved. Are you sure I'm not imposing?"

"Positive."

I climbed into his Ford F-150 truck. "Nice vehicle," I said, impressed.

"Comes in handy and there's just something about a truck. Know what I mean?" His eyes questioned me.

"Yes, I know what you mean."

Did I? There was a sense of power in the roar of the big engine, a certain masculinity in the bigness of the machine, perhaps to what he was referring.

We rode in silence except for the noise of the engine. Howard made turns from one unmarked gravel road onto another then another. "I'm glad I'm with you. I could never find my way back to the apartment."

Howard laughed. "Yeah, I know this country like the back of my hand. I couldn't get lost even if I tried. We're getting together on the old Miller farm. The land hasn't been worked for a couple of years. Jessie can make a better living trucking long hauls. He's out of town at the moment but he's given us permission. In fact, we've used it so frequently the place looks like a park. We have picnic tables, horseshoe rings and seating for a dozen or so.

Well, we're here," he said as he brought the truck to a halt and turned off the big engine.

Around us were several vehicles parked at random and people moving about. A dozen children ran about tagging one another. As we climbed from the truck, Summer broke away from the others and walked toward us.

"Hi, Howard," she said as she lifted her cheek for his light kiss.

She turned toward me. "Hello, Harley. I'm glad you could join us." She pushed back her dark hair. She was just as beautiful as I remembered."Thank you for inviting me." We joined the others.

A fire was already crackling in a pit, sending bright orange bits into the air.

"Everybody, this here's Harley Daniels, a friend of ours." Howard spoke loudly, so everyone could hear.

"Hey Harley, welcome."

"Hi."

"Nice to meet you."

The crowd had all spoken at once but each had clearly been friendly. I waved and smiled in return. Howard had forgotten to introduce me as reverend which was an easy mistake since I had removed my collar.

Maybe it would be better to drop my role as reverend for awhile, especially during the investigation. When people noticed my collar they always seemed to develop a reserve as if they didn't feel free to be themselves. Yes, I decided, for the next two months I would simply be Harley.

My vocation along with my pastoral attire would be quietly stored in the closet.

A long wooden table was laden with food: vegetables, salads, desserts and melon slices. I'm sure my jaw dropped as I eyed the fare. "Wow," I declared.

"See, I told you there'd be enough for guests. This is eastern Kentucky, always enough for everybody."

Howard handed me a pocket knife. "Here, make yourself useful. We need some forked sticks cut for the wieners."

I stood clutching the knife, not quite sure what was expected of me. "Come on Harley, we'll help you," said a youth standing close by.

"This way." He pointed to a thicket not far away. "There are some young hickories growing over there. They will be perfect."

"Yeah Harley, we'll help you," another child added. Soon I was surrounded by children with excited voices.

"Okay, let's go get those wiener sticks." My voice lifted along with my mood. I loved kids. Beth and I planned to have lots of children, however many God should bless us with. For now though, I would enjoy the blessings bestowed on other parents. I joined the game of selecting just the right small sapling limbs where they forked into smaller parts then with a pocket knife, cut them to proper lengths.

"See, that's where we put the wiener and hold it over the fire," one of my helpers said.

"That's very clever," I replied.

"You mean, you ain't never roasted wieners?" the youth asked, his eyes wide with disbelief.

"You mean, have never," I corrected, ruffling his yellow hair straw-like hair..

"That's what I said." We all laughed, picked up our pile of wiener sticks and headed back to the others.

The sun had fallen below the horizon, sending out red and orange rays and distant shadows were forming when we gathered around the fire and roasted our hot dogs. I watched as the meats plumped then dripped little juice droplets into the embers as they browned. The flames brightened the faces around me to amber hues. We sang silly songs and shared knock- knock jokes then filled our plates with other good eats.

I couldn't remember food tasting so good.

After we had eaten and the ladies had packed the food away, we all piled onto a wagon heaped high with hay. An old red tractor would pull us. "Hey Roy, did you bring your banjo?" Howard asked a tall, lanky guy of about sixty years.

"It's in my truck," the man returned. He jumped from the wagon and soon returned with an ancient five string instrument. The tractor inched forward as the man lightly strummed the strings. Contentment settled over me as I listened to the putt- putt of the tractor engine and the musical accompaniment, a feeling so deep it seemed to reach my very soul.

Nearby, Summer leaned in closer to Howard and he dropped a kiss on her upturned lips. A pang of jealousy pierced my heart. No, my mind recoiled, not jealousy but envy. I missed having Beth at my side.

I would like to have been holding her, sharing this remarkable experience and these wonderful people with the woman I loved.

"What would you like to hear?" the man with the banjo asked.

"What should he play, Harley?" someone asked.

Everybody waited with their eyes on me. I thought of a tune I heard on the car radio on my way east. "Do you know, *I've Got a Mule to Ride*?"

"Fine choice, Harley," he said.

"You all can help me on this one."

His fingers flew across the strings at lightning speed. I had chosen a fast paced piece. He chanted the rhythmic verse.

I've got a mule to ride, I've got a mule to ride, ain't got no saddle but I'm rarin' to ride. When he came to the part, *said the duck to the drake,* we all chanted, *quack, quack, quack, quack."*

The ring from my cell phone vibrated from the pocket of the shirt I had purchased. I raised the device to my ear. "Hello," I said.

"Hello, Harley? Is that you? I can hardly hear you. What is all that noise?"

"Hi, Beth," I said to my wife. "That's a banjo you hear, and a tractor, and kids. We're singing."

"Harley, where are you and what on earth are you doing?"

"I'm on a hay ride and having great fun. Did you get to your mother's house safely?" I raised my voice above the din around me.

"Yes, I'm at Mother's." Beth's voice trailed off as if she didn't know what to say next. We had never had an uncomfortable silence between us, never. Sadness swelled inside me. "Well, I just wanted to make sure you traveled safely."

"I'm fine. Say hello to your mother for me. Take care." I lowered my voice. "I love you."

"All right, keep in touch."

Beth had not responded to my endearment. She was still mad. A lump rose in my throat. With a sigh, I closed my phone and slipped it back into my new used plaid shirt pocket.

"Come on, Harley, sing," the child who sat closest to me yelled. I joined in the chorus. *I've got a mule to ride. I've got a mule to ride. Ain't got no saddle but I'm rarin' to ride.*

Chapter Eleven

The light of dawn was filtering through the window when I awoke. I lay on my side with my arms clutching a pillow. I had unknowingly pulled the polyester filled cushion close at some point during the night. Not having Beth beside me tore at my heart. The pillow was a poor substitute so I pushed it away.

I rose and sat on the side of the bed. I had slept well in spite of my circumstance. This would be the first day of my investigation. A feeling of inadequacy engulfed me. I needed help. "God," I said aloud. "What do I do next?" I waited for divine guidance. My words echoed in the silent room. "I guess I'm on my own for now. God, please be there if I get in trouble."

I knew where I was going today, Jasper, where the murder had been committed then on to the badlands. I wanted to see the scene of the crime.

I needed to view the characters who played a role in Woody's demise. Faceless figures who hovered in my mind would be brought to life.

After a quick shower I donned my other jeans and shirt. I inspected my appearance in the mirror hanging above the sink. I had forgotten to pack my shaver and it was time for a haircut. Why should I care how I looked? I would see no one I knew. Quickly, I was shedding the appearance of a man of the cloth.

Better for my undercover work, I decided.

Gratitude swelled inside me as I consumed the coffee and rolls Howard had provided. With my notebook under my arm and a cup of coffee in my hand, I descended the steps from the apartment. Howard was already at work changing a tire.

"Where you headed," he asked.

"I thought I might as well get started on this investigation. I'll be driving up to the scene of the murder in Jasper and then visit the club where Carrie worked.

Howard stopped work and stood with his hands on his hips. "Well, you be careful. I've heard there's some pretty rough dudes up there. Do you want me to come with you?" he asked, concern in his voice.

"No, no, I don't intend to cause any trouble."

The thought of Howard at six feet three inches at my side was a reassuring thought.

"Call me if you need anything. Just keep in mind that it'll take me a couple of hours to get to you."

"Thanks, Howard, for everything."

With a wave of my hand, I pulled out of Howard's lot onto the narrow road. A map lay unfolded on the seat beside me.

I could shorten my trip by traveling a portion of the way by interstate but chose instead the more scenic back roads. The morning sky was gray and overcast with the threat of rain. I realized Ishould have checked the weather forecast before beginning my trip but I doubted if the forecast of a storm would have deterred me today.

The road was winding and narrow. Mostly my view was limited to the twisting road in front of me. Occasionally on the top of a rise I could slow my vehicle and see lush deep hollows.

The sky kept darkening. I knew a storm was brewing and would erupt soon. I began to grow bored with the sameness of the drive. I drove through several small lifeless burgs, each with their fast food stores.

Finally, I saw a small rectangular wooden sign, announcing my arrival in 'Jasper'. I slowed as I entered the small town. I was ready for a break.

Most of the store fronts seemed to have empty spaces behind dark windows. A few vehicles sat about but no one stirred, probably because of the impending storm.

The sky had turned blue-black. Street lights had come on, casting an eerie glow over broken pavement and closed doors with peeling paint.

Before I knew it, I was on the other side of town. My eyes were searching for the Starlight Motel. The storm was breaking with dangerous streaks of lightning and a fierce wind when I spotted the long dingy white cinder-block building.

At least blue shutters had been added to break the bleakness of the structure. I pulled into the gravel parking lot just as the slashing rain began.

The storm was so intense I felt I was witnessing the wrath of God.

With each roll of thunder, He spoke to my heart.

"Thou shall not kill"

"Yes, Lord." I bowed my head in submission.

"I made you in my image. I am disgraced daily. How much more can I endure."

"Yes, Lord. I'm so sorry."

I apologized for the failings of my fellow man.

"I gave you the precious gift of life and everything to fulfill your needs."

"Yes, Lord, you did. I'm sorry. I'm so thankful, so very thankful for your blessings. There are many, many hearts who thank you, Lord. Good people who revere you and love their fellow man."

Suddenly the storm ceased as if God's burst of anger had passed. I lifted my head. The rain had washed away the dust from the motel leaving it fresh and clean. If only the crime that had been committed inside its walls could as easily be washed away. The units numbered ten just like the owner had said in the trial. I counted over to number five.

"That's where Carrie was killed," I whispered to myself. How could a place that had seen such violence appear so ordinary? Somehow the room should be different than the others, stained maybe, eternally marked, a reminder of the inhuman actions of someone.

I climbed from my vehicle and headed for the door marked 'office'. I stepped inside. A desk sat in the middle of the small space, flanked by a couple of worn chairs. A bell sat on the desk with a sign that read, 'ring for service', so I did.

An elderly man shuffled into the room. He was thin with stooped shoulders; perhaps in his seventies.

There's one suspect I can take off my list, I thought. A young woman like Carrie could never be overpowered by this old man. She could have folded him like a towel.

"What can I do for you, young man," he inquired.

"I'm investigating the murder that was committed here in room five. Would you be kind enough to allow me entry to the room to look around?"

The old guy drew the corners of his mouth down in a grimace. "The cops already been over that room with a fine tooth comb. There ain't no evidence left."

"Just the same I'd like to see for myself."

"Oh, you would, would you? I done cleaned that room, had to buy a new mattress and new carpet. Cost me a pretty penny, too. I tell ye there ain't nothin' there.

If you want to see that room so bad, I'll let it to you for thirty-five dollars a night."

"I don't want to spend the night," I protested.

"Take it or leave it, I got things to do."

I hesitated. The need in me to see where Carrie died won. I pulled out my wallet. "Do you take credit cards?" I asked.

He gave me a scathing rake with his gaze. "Does a dog bark?"

I handed him my card and he placed it in a small machine and imprinted it on a paper. "Sign here," he said with a scowl.

I did as I was told. He handed me my card, a signed copy and a key. "Be out by noon tomorrow," he said, then turned his back to leave the room.

What a guy, I thought. What kind of life must he have suffered to turn him into this unhappy, grouchy old man.

"God bless you," I was inspired to call after him. He hesitated but didn't turn around to answer.

I walked the few feet to room #5 and opened the door.

I didn't know what I expected, something should have been different, not just another cheap motel room. The walls were streaked with cheap green paint. It was sparsely appointed with twin beds covered with faded printed covers, a cabinet with an old TV atop, side tables next to the beds and in a corner, a round table with two padded chairs.

I would not get any clues here.

I had wasted thirty-five dollars. Wearied by the storm and a little tired from the trip, I decided to lay down on one of the beds and rest. I closed my eyes; I may as well catch a nap since I had until noon tomorrow.

She came to me in a dream, first the fragrance, a sweet little girl smell of talc and flowers. *That's the fragrance of an angel,* I thought. She hovered above me, a beautiful girl with an ivory complexion, red-blond hair billowed around her face. *Milk and honey, how apt,* I thought.

I tried to speak. "Carrie, is that you?" The experience was surreal. I tried to awaken.

She placed her finger to her lips as if to hush me. "Read my thesis," she whispered, her voice light as a feather.

"What?"

"Read my thesis." She smiled and her face glowed radiant like sunshine. Then she was gone.

"Don't go, Carrie," I pleaded. "Please come back."

I awoke suddenly and she wasn't there. I wondered what had just happened. Had I witnessed a visitor from the afterlife? I totally believed in the spirit world.

I really saw the essence of Carrie, why didn't she just tell me who killed her. That would have made everything much easier. "Who killed you, Carrie?" I asked aloud.

Into my mind came an answer. She didn't know; she didn't know who brutally slashed her throat. "I'm sorry, Carrie, of course he would have been masked and gloved. I will find that monster and bring him to justice, I promise you."

Had she given me a clue? 'Check my thesis,' she had said. I'm sure the police would have gone over all her writings and her computer, but I would make another search.

My stomach growled, reminding me it was well past lunch time. I walked outside. A young man in an orange jumpsuit was sweeping the sidewalk.

"Excuse me, Sir." He turned at my raised call.

"Yeah, whatcha' want?"

"Is there a good place to get a meal around here?"

"You mean, like a restaurant?"

He scratched his head as if thinking. "Nope, ain't no restaurant here.

Oh," he seemed to have a second thought. "There's a deli at the Market. You can get fried chicken, mashed potatoes, stuff like that."

"That sounds wonderful. Where is the Market?"

He pointed. "On up the road a ways; ain't far."

"Thank you," I said.

He was right; the store wasn't far.

The 'Market' was appropriately named, stocked with groceries, movie rentals, nails and lumber. Anything a person might have need of on a regular basis.

In the back I saw a lighted 'deli' sign.

An older woman in a white apron stood behind a case full of good stick- to your- ribs food. She had a friendly smiling face and gray hair pulled up inside a hair net.

"Hi, young man, what can I get you?"

I smiled at her. "It's hard to make up my mind. Everything looks so good."

"Just take your time," she said as she tucked a strand of gray hair up under the heavy net. "You got your pick of a meat, two veggies and bread for $3.99."

"That's a great price."

"Are you visiting family or something?"

"No," I said, "just passing through. I've got a room over at the Starlight Motel. I'll have the chicken breast, mashed potatoes, and corn please, oh, and one of those homemade biscuits."

"Sorry we don't have any better accommodations than that motel. It's just a place for riff-raff that's headed for the gentlemen's clubs.

There's a bunch of them just over the state line."

Her face reddened, "I'm sorry, I didn't mean to offend you. You look like a fine young man."

"Thank you, I am," I smiled. "No offense taken." I thought I would get the local take on Carrie's murder. I was sure the friendly lady would be more than happy to oblige. "I heard about a murder committed there last year."

"Yes, the poor girl! I think she was working in one of those clubs."

"Did they get the murderer?"

"I don't think so.

"Oh, they arrested her boyfriend, prosecuted him, too. But I don't think they got the right person. I'd say she got too close to something.

Drugs flow around here like creek water. There's some mighty bad dealers around that place."

She snapped the Styrofoam container together. "That'll be $4.23, young man. There's some tables right over there," she said, pointing, then she took my money. "Pop's in the vending machine."

"Thanks."

Was pop all people drank around here? I wondered. I did find bottled iced tea in the machine. Thankfully, I retrieved the drink.

The food was great and I ate heartily but all the time my mind was anxious to move on up the road to the badlands. Before long I was back under the wheel.

The road was narrow and twisting. Soon I entered the area where the gentlemen's clubs were located. A building with paint-blackened windows was first to draw my attention.

The name in big bold neon flashed at me, Lady Godiva, it read, accompanied by a picture of a buxom young lady with strategically placed falling blond hair.

I was surprised to find a Dollar Store nearby and a Mc Donalds restaurant not far. The town, in fact, was much like the others with two churches and a police station.

The next conspicuous building had no windows. A sign said Girls, Girls, Girls, Topless and Anxious to Please. I drove slowly past another couple of dark buildings with gaudy bright lights suggesting delightful beauties inside. I was searching for the Fantasy Nights club but so far I hadn't found it. I drove on until I had passed through the settlement. Finally, I saw it, a large building painted black. My heart started thumping. Encircling the top was a band of golden stars. It was off the road with a private drive that led to a large parking lot.

As I drove through the entrance I had the feeling I was being watched.

All was quiet so I drove up to get a closer look at the structure. A large poster was plastered to the wall close by the door. See Shapely Shaw at eight. There she was, the girl from the trial transcript.

The picture was a larger than life image so I studied the girl. She had a pretty face but not beautiful. Her best feature was her eyes.

They were blue but with brown circling the irises and fanning out through the bright blue orbs. Her hair was blond and fell in full waves to her shoulders. She held her mouth in a pout, reminding me of photos of a famous actress of the fifties. I hoped I got the opportunity to meet Miss Shapely Shaw.

I drove around the building noting it was a cinder- block structure of at least ten thousand square feet. Three rear entrance doors lined the back. There was a more elaborate entrance in front with tall white pillars and a solid red door. I sighed.

Had I expected more? I had thought I would feel elation when finally I saw the club but instead I just had a feeling of unease in my stomach. My investigation was taking me into uncharted territory. As I pulled back onto the highway I felt like I had left a dark place and knew that although it brought me chills, I would reenter it again soon.

Chapter Twelve

The parking lot was crowded with vehicles. I had to circle to find a place to park. The stars around the top of the Fantasy Nights club glowed golden. Music drummed, muffled by the block and mortar walls.

Men were lined up at the entrance. Briefly, I hesitated. I was a man of the cloth, about to enter a place cursed by my beliefs. "God," I said, "you know this is not where I would choose to be had it not been for Woody and poor Carrie. I feel I must find justice for them both. Please be with me."

I took my place in line and pulled out my wallet. I saw the other guys were clutching $10's so I pulled out a bill.

"Stiff cover charge, ain't it, the beefy man in front of me said as he glanced over his shoulder."But it's worth it," he added.

"It's worth it just to see Shapely. She sure is something. They bring her on at 8:00, that way the working Johns get a chance to see her.

We're a hard working bunch and just can't handle that 2 AM stuff. Gotta get some sleep on a weeknight. What do you do?" he asked.

"I'm . . . . . .I'm a . . . ."

"Hey, Pete, I figured you'd be here."

Another man ran up and slapped the fellow on the shoulder. Pete answered his friend, forgetting that I had not answered his question, to my relief.

What would I have said?

How could I answer if I were asked again? I'm not working right now. Yes, that would be enough said. It was just an idle question anyhow.

I handed the burly guy at the ticket counter my money and stuck out my hand, palm down, like I watched the other men do. I received an ink stamp. I looked at the black mark on the back of my hand, almost expecting a 666 imprinted on me instead it was the current date.

The lights were low so my eyes adjusted slowly. On a stage a band of musicians beat at their instruments, so loudly, I felt like putting my hands over my ears. I thought, now, how cool would that be? A wooden bar stretched along one wall, the lower section was covered with tacky red velvet. Two scantily-clad female bartenders were already serving up drinks.

Lighted poles stretched from the floor of the stage to the ceiling but no dancers were performing yet. A red velvet curtain served as a backdrop.

"Hey, Cutie." I felt a tap on my shoulder.

A young woman with very red hair stood there clutching a bottle in her hand. "First beer is on the house," she said with a very white smile.

"Thank you," I said, not allowing my gaze to fall to the ample bosom she had half exposed in a skimpy garment.

"My name is Roxie. If you need anything, just you let me know, Baby." She winked then walked away with an exaggerated sway of her hips to get lost in the crowd.

I was surprised to see women customers in the club. I had assumed there would be only men but a few sat at tables scattered about the room. Their laughter pealed through the air. Smoke rose from lighted cigarettes.

Soon the place would be dense with a white fog. I stood ill at ease in the crowded room. I didn't know where to stand or what to do so I took a drink of my beer. I never drink but saw nothing wrong with an occasional beer or a glass of wine. I worked my way off the crowded floor and stood against a wall. From that vantage point I could observe the crowd. I was searching for a killer.

Someone in this establishment was probably a murderer. The guilty party would not readily expose his crime.

Surely one could not do such a hideous act without guilt affecting him in some manner. Surely some action would be telling to an aware observer.

The room became more crowded and the smoke got thicker; the people became louder. I took another sip from my bottle. The beer had become warm.

A gentleman seemed to be working his way toward me. Was I going to get bounced, reproached for not visiting the bar?

"How's it going?" he asked.

"All right," I answered.

"You look about as comfortable as I feel." He grinned a little crookedly.

"Does it show that badly?"

"Yes, it does," he answered and again smiled. "I'm Max, short for Maxwell, Max Holmes." He stretched out his smooth hand for a shake.

"I'm Harley Daniels."

"Nice to meet you, Harley."

He studied me then said, "If you don't mind me asking, what are you doing in this place? You don't fit."

"You don't seem to fit either," I returned. He had a clean-cut look about him, neat haircut, trimmed mustache, nice clothes, topped with a sports jacket. He looked professional, like a character in a James Bond movie.

"I'm just nosing around," he said "I'd heard a lot about this place and thought I'd check it out, thought there might be a story here. I'm a freelance reporter/writer. I write for newspapers, magazines, some e-news and, of course, I also have this book in the back of my head that I intend to write. What about you?"

There it was, the question. My eyes met his. He waited for my response. Could I trust this stranger? His eyes were clear and met mine squarely.

Why not, I thought. "I'm a preacher."

He laughed. "Are you serious? If you try to start saving souls in here, they'll toss you out on your ear."

"Oh, I'm not trying to save souls. I mean, I would if I could but that's not why I'm here."

He waited expectantly.

"I . . . . I'm here to see Shapely Shaw, the exotic dancer with the big red X."

He raised his brows.

Too late I realized I had quoted the trial transcript. I had to explain. "It's a long story. I'll tell you about it if you have the time."

"Like I said, I'm looking for a story." He motioned to Roxie to bring two more bottles. "Let's find a table. We'll be able to get one in the back. The show is about to begin."

"Bring on the girls." The crowd was beginning to get rowdy.

We seated ourselves in red velvet covered chairs. Who had decorated this place? I thought in distaste. I took a sip from my fresh cold beer.

"Well, Preacher?" He looked at me with searching eyes.

I took a deep breath and began telling him Woody's story.

"Hold on," he said as he felt around his jacket pockets. I knew what he was looking for and retrieved my new journal from my pants pocket and handed it to him. "Thanks," he said. He clicked his pen and began writing. "Go on, what happened next?"

I related to him everything that had happened to date, the murder, Woody's trial, and my subsequent investigation.

"Wow, that's quite a story," Max said. "There's just one thing wrong."

"It doesn't have an ending." He appeared thoughtful, rubbing his chin.

"Not yet," I said, but I'm not giving up.

There has to be an answer here." I peered around the room. Wild would not quite describe the scene or the people. If ever there was a place where a murderer could hide it was here.

"Do you mind if I hang around to see the conclusion of your investigation?" Max asked."This is the most interesting subject I've discovered of late."

almost an answered prayer

"I'd like that. You could be kind of like a partner." It was good to have someone share my experience. I was beginning to feel my aloneness. "Have you been in this club before?" I turned my attention back to the reasons for my being there.

"Yes, a couple of times. Why do you ask?"

"Do you know a character named Juan Manos?"

"Yes, he's South American, I think; a bad looking dude if you ask me. He's always showing off his big bills. I've heard most wise people make a point to stay out of his way.

"Could you point him out to me?" I asked.

"In this crowd? I don't know." Max stood and craned his neck. "He's usually where the girls are. Come on, let's walk over that way and I'll see if he's here." Max lifted himself from his chair and carried his bottle of beer. I followed close behind him. The crowd had thickened and gotten noisier on that end of the floor. The girls who had been dancing on the poles had exited the stage and were moving among the male patrons. The emcee took the mike.

"How'd you like that dancing, guys." He held up his hand to halt the yells and whistles. "Well, it's tip time. Show these young ladies how much you appreciate them and be respectful. You know my bouncers don't stand for no rough stuff." He gave a knowing laugh.

Thumping music began anew. I watched in shocked disbelief as the men tucked bills beneath skimpy attire.

Their fingers, deliberate and slow against the skin close to the private areas of the young girls' bodies.

My heart hurt at the actions I was witnessing: I had to turn away.

Burly men stood guard allowing only what the girls allowed. The larger the bill, the more access the man got; the longer his hand was allowed to remain.

I wanted to throw up my hand and cry, "Stop, stop, in the name of God, stop, but instead I closed my eyes and turned away. The noise, smoke, skin, and laughter closed in on me. I wiped my eyes as if I could wipe away the scene in front of me.

Max placed a hand on my shoulder. "You could never stop this, Preacher." He hesitated a moment then said. "Do you still want to see Juan Manos?"

"Yes," I opened my eyes. I had to see him for myself.

"Well, he's right over there." Max pointed as discreetly as possible.

The man was large. His olive skin shone with perspiration and his black oiled hair hung long. He sat staring at the dancer who was twisting and gyrating on her knees atop his table, a young woman, about nineteen.Still a child, an innocent, I thought.

She should be in a dorm room somewhere, not witness to such depravity. In one hand he grasped $100 bills, his other hand was hidden beneath the table. My stomach churned.Three other men of the same nationality stood around as if to watch his back. One turned and his eyes met mine.

His facial features were thick and unattractive, his gaze, hard and unfeeling.

Darkness hid his emotions and his secrets. I knew he had them.

"Those are his goons," Max said of the three."Seen enough?" he asked.

I nodded my head. We made our way back to the farthest corner. I had definitely seen enough. There was just nothing right about this place.

This was the Devil's playground and I was in its midst. The music was beating at my head. I wanted to run and never return.

"It's almost eight," Max said, glancing at his watch.

"What?" My mind was numb from what I had witnessed.

"Eight. That's when Shapely takes the stage. You wanted to see her, remember?"

"Oh yes, the girl from the trial, the girl on the billboard with the beautiful eyes, I had almost forgotten the reason I was there. "I don't know if I can tolerate any more of this, Max."

"We'll keep our distance. You can hardly see the stage from here."

He was right. From our perspective there was just a blur of noise and lights. I sat down and tried to recoup.

"Another fresh cold beer will help," Max said. He raised his hand and instantly Roxie was there with two cold drinks.

My head had begun to throb.

The pain must have shown on my face for the girl asked, "Something wrong, Honey?"

"My head, it hurts. Could I get a couple of aspirins, please?"

"Sorry, Sugar, we don't serve aspirin but I can fix that headache." She placed our drinks on the table and grabbed me gently by the shoulders and pulled me back in my chair. She massaged her hands around the base of my neck and over my shoulders. "Man, you're tense. Just relax." She continued to apply pressure, working around my shoulders and down my spine. My body began to relax and the headache soon faded.

"Roxie," I said, "you're very good at this."

"Yes, I know. I'll soon have my degree then I'll be a master masseuse." She sighed longingly.

"Will you be leaving the club?" Max asked her.

"You bet," she said emphatically then hurriedly added, "don't get me wrong, this place is okay. The money's good but it's not a career, if you know what I mean. I plan on working at one of those fancy spas and maybe one day, who knows, perhaps I'll have my own place."

"Well, I thank you for your services. I'm sure you'll go far in your field," I said as I moved my head from side to side with new ease.

"Are many of the girls going to school on the side?" Max inquired.

"A few," Roxie replied, "But some of them like this kind of life."

"What about Shapely Shaw?

What does she want to do with her life?" Max was acting like the reporter he was.

Roxie laughed. "Shapely wants to be a star, you know, big time. She's always talking about being in the movies and posing in Playboy and that kind of stuff."

I glanced to the distant stage. The lights were low but I could see the figure twisting and turning, not quite like the other girls. Shapely seemed to have grace and skill, more like a professional dancer and only partially nude. She seemed to have had some training.

Max pulled out his wallet and retrieved some folded money. "Roxie, would you get a message to Shapely?" He handed the bills to the girl.

"Sure, be happy to." She tucked the money in her bra.

"What's the message?"

"I'm a writer and I submit to Playboy. Tell her I'd like to do a story on her."

With a twist of her body and a flounce of her short skirt Roxie disappeared in the crowd.

I looked at my new friend and knew my mouth had fallen open.

"You wanted to talk to Shapely, didn't you?" he asked with a grin. Then he burst with laughter like he was privy to a joke.

"Yes, yes," I stuttered. I could feel my cheeks flushing like a kid.

"Oh man, I need my camera. I left it in my car." He rose from his chair. "I do my own photos," he added. "I won't be gone long."

"But . . . but what about Shapely?"

"If she gets here before I get back then you can talk to her."

"Alright," I said, with a break in my voice. I was nervous, but why? She was just a woman as any other. I was usually at ease with everyone; saw each as a child of God, to be respected and loved. I was not a naive teenager and I would not act like one.

Chapter Thirteen

I turned uneasily in my chair. Shapely was no longer on stage. My gaze searched the room. Roxie was a tall girl so I spotted her red head. She was talking to someone and pointing my way. My heart picked up pace. A curvy blond began making her way through the crowd. It was Shapely.

She stopped at my table. "Hi there," she said in a voice with a breathless affection. "Do you want to see me?"

"Yes, yes," I said.

"Are you a writer?"Shapely asked pointedly."Can you get me in Playboy?"

"Oh, no, that's my friend, Max. He went to his car to get his camera."

"Oh," she said, rolling her eyes. "That's a pretty good line, Mister. I fell for it."

Her voice dropped the breathless sound and now showed a definite rural twang. Her body slumped to a more relaxed state. I realized she had been holding a pose.

"I apologize. Max is really a photo journalist. "He has really gone to get his camera . . . I swear." I raised my hand like I was in court.

She folded her arms across her chest, evidently not impressed, and patted her foot on the floor impatiently.

"My name is Harley Daniels."

I stuck out my hand then drew it back when she didn't respond. "I'm investigating the murder of Carrie Ann on behalf of Woody Pierce. Max and I just happened to meet here."

"Oh?" I seemed to have peaked her interest. "Are you one of those private eye people, like in the movies?"

"That's exactly what I am." I decided I was indeed a private investigator. "Please sit down." I pulled out a chair. "Please."

"All right," she said with a pout. But this Max fellow better show up and he better have a camera." She adjusted her clothes as she sat down, pulling her top low and tight over her bosom which extended out over the table. I lowered my gaze away from her. She noticed my actions.

"What's the matter? Don't you think I'm pretty?"

She fluffed her hair and I felt forced to lift my gaze to meet hers.

"Yes, you have beautiful eyes. Their image should be framed and hung in a gallery."

She hesitated, then smiled. "Thank you, how flattering. I have my grandmother's eyes on my daddy's side. People don't usually notice my eyes. They see everything else."

"Well they should. It's their loss."

Shapely smiled. She and I would be friends, this I knew.

It was in the eyes. "So, how come you're doing this private eye stuff? It sounds dangerous."

"It's a long story and yes I suppose it can be quite dangerous."

She leaned over and whispered secretively, "Poor Carrie. I've been thinking, Woody just couldn't have killed . . . like that, not with the throat cut and all that. I didn't know how she was done in when I was testifying at the trial. Woody could have killed her by accident, maybe if he slapped her too hard and maybe broke her neck.

I've heard of that happening, but not with no knife, not that. He would never do it on purpose." She shuddered. "I'll help your investigation all I can."

"You know that if Woody didn't do it then someone who knew Carrie killed her, maybe someone she knew here at the club."

"Gee." Shapely's expressive eyes grew larger. "Someone here? I might know a killer? I hadn't thought of that."

"Yes, I think it's very likely, considering her exposure here to unsavory elements."

She leaned in closely again."There are some hard eggs who come in here."

"Great shot!"

Max had flashed his camera at an inappropriate time. He flashed again when we glanced up.

Max laughed. "Got you, Preacher."

Shapely gave me a sharp look.

"Preacher! You're a preacher?"

"Yes," I admitted, a bit sheepishly, "but I'm working undercover."

"I'm Maxwell Holmes, Max to my friends." With a wide grin he reached his hand toward Shapely.

Shapely touched his hand lightly. "And just what are you really?" she directed at him, her voice dripping with skepticism.

"I'm a writer, a photojournalist to be more exact."

"Let me get this straight." She pointed to me. "You are a preacher who's working undercover as a private investigator. And you," she turned her pointing finger to Max, "are a writer who works freelance."

"Yes," Max and I answered together.

Shapely giggled. "This is crazy but I believe you so what about Playboy?"

"You're too good for Playboy," Max said in a familiar tone. "I've got better things in mind." He gave her a wink.

"What?" she asked pointedly but she couldn't hide the excitement in her voice.

"Trust me," he said with a smile. "I promise you won't be sorry." He pulled out the notebook I had loaned him earlier. "How long have you worked here?" he asked, "and how long with Carrie?"

Shapely readily answered his questions, giving him all the information I wanted to gather.

"How many rooms are there in the club, Shapely?" Max changed the direction of his questions.

"I'm not sure. There are rest rooms off the hallway and one large room for the girls to change clothes. I have my own small dressing room as did Carrie. I know there's a room for the band members and Mr. Wallace, the manager, has an office.

I think the rest is stock room but I'm not sure. Oh, we performers have our own entrance but there are others." She hesitated, "There is one other room but I'd rather not talk about it."

Max didn't push her, just said, "That leaves a lot of unexplained area. This is quite a large building. Who owns the Fantasy Nights Club?" Max asked.

Shapely hesitated. "I really don't know. Mr. Wallace takes care of all the business; he orders the alcohol, pays us and the band and all that stuff but I don't think he owns the club."

"Who have you seen frequent Mr. Wallace's office; someone who acts like he belongs there, someone that no one questions?" Max probed.

"Oh, that would be Juan Manos, but he just has so much money that he gets anything he wants. I don't think he owns the place, he just acts like he does."

"H-m-m-m-m, the mystery deepens," Max said. "Preacher, are you taking all this in?"

"Yes," I said. "I need to find out who owns the place. Could we see your dressing room, Shapely?" I asked.

"I don't know," she said uneasily.

"We're not allowed to have men in the dressing rooms. I could get in trouble."

"We'll be careful," Max said. "Did you say your room is down the hall from the men's room?"

"Yes, my door has a gold star on it."

"That's because you're the star, Baby."

Max pinched her chin in a playful manner and she beamed.

We three sat there as if to ask, "What next?"

"Where did Carrie stay when she worked here?" Max asked.

"She had her room too; it was in the corner where the hallway turns." Shapely answered.

"But it's locked, ever since the killing. Somebody put a padlock on the door and nobody goes near as far as I know."

"Strange," I said.

"Yeah, boys I have to leave," Shapely said, glancing at her watch.

"We have to talk more, Shapely. Will you give me your phone number?"

Her eyes flashed between Max and me.

"Yes, my cell number." She reached for Max's pad. "You can call me anytime. I really want to find justice for Carrie."

We watched as she retraced her steps through the throng of unruly patrons. She stepped carefully, avoiding reaching hands. She maintained a smile for the rowdy men.

"What now?" Max asked.

"Well, first thing is to relieve myself of this beer." I said, noting the uncomfortable state of my abdomen.

"Yeah, me too. Follow me. The men's room is down the hall a ways."

We were washing our hands and Max was checking out the room. "This place is really cheaply constructed."

"Really? How can you tell?"

I knew nothing about construction. "Look at the ceiling," he said, "just a framework with drop-in panels

I bet they're attached to the rafters, probably an open loft."

"So?" I questioned the importance of his observation.

"We could probably climb up there and have access to the whole place. Come on."

Within a stall, he climbed up on a commode tank and lifted a panel then peeked inside. "Just as I thought, come on follow me." He lunged then pulled himself up and out of sight.

I followed. The area was dark but slivers of light crept through cracks in the ceiling. Max replaced the panel he had laid aside.

"It's warm up here," I said.

"S-h-h-h-h." He hushed me. We crawled monkey-style across the structure. The noise and voices alerted us to which area lay below us. Max pointed and mouthed the word *office*. I followed him, making sure I was quiet. I was beginning to see the possible aid to my investigation. "Come on in, Shapely," the manager of the club said in a gravelly voice.

"I have your check ready. You put on a good show tonight."

Feminine footsteps clicked across the floor. "Thank you, Mr. Wallace."

"You know, Juan would like some personal attention from you which would increase your take-home considerably."

"No, absolutely not. I've told you before; I don't get touched especially by Juan Manos."

Shapely's voice rose in anger.

"He gives me the creeps and his men give me the creeps too. Why are they around so much? Do they own this place?"

Mr. Wallace huffed, "The ownership of this club is not to be known, so don't ever ask again."

"All right, all right, I won't inquire again."

"I noticed you were out on the floor with some customers," the manager growled."

They were just guys, unusual pair, they're here to…"

"No, Shapely, no. Don't tell, please." I whispered.

"To do what?" the manager demanded.

Shapely hesitated. "They were photographers and wanted photos of me for Playboy."

"Thanks, Shapely." I muttered under my breath.

"Remember your contract, Shapely. Anything you do has to be handled by the club. You signed your life away, girl, for the next two years at least."

"Yeah, I forgot, but after two years I'm out of here."

"Whew, that lets me off the hook," Max breathed low.

We made our way over the rafters listening to the noise below. "This should be about where Carrie's room was located." Max whispered.

"Just a minute." He drew a deep sharp breath as he pulled on a string and lifted out a small circular piece of ceiling.

"Someone else has been up here," he gasped, "a peeping tom. Someone had been watching Carrie."

"That's sick," I said

"Yeah, a person that sick could also turn into a murderer. Just think, he watches her and builds this fantasy of desire for her and she rejects him; giant motive."

"A perfect motive, maybe we're getting somewhere after all."

"Let's see what else we can find." Max said with a sigh. I followed him carefully through the darkened space. Below we heard the clicking of feminine heels. A door opened then closed. "Darn that Mr. Wallace."

"Shapely." Max and I mouthed at the same time.

"This must be her dressing room," he said.

We crawled until we were directly over her. "Oh God," Max breathed then whispered, "I'm sorry, Preacher, I don't use the Lord's name lightly. "I had a good reason. Look." He pulled another string attached to a small piece of ceiling tile.

"That same pervert has been looking at Shapely too."

"Oh no. If this man is a murderer, Shapely could be in danger.

She could be next. What are we going to do? We have to let her know." I could feel panic rising inside me.

"Keep a cool head, Preacher. We don't know if the two crimes are related." We crawled back to where we had entered and dropped back down into the men's room."We've got to think this thing through."

"I guess you're right," I agreed. "But I'm still worried about Shapely. We need to tell her she's being spied on." Max rubbed his chin thoughtfully.

"If we do that, she'll run directly to the manager and complain, and there will go our cover and our hidden listening post. We really need that loft area. If there's anything to learn in this place, we'll hear it up there."

"You're right," I reluctantly agreed. "I'll say a prayer for her safety though; that's the least I can do."

"That's fine, Preacher but can you do it a little later? I think we'd better leave this place. If we don't start doing some serious drinking and hugging up the ladies we're going to look conspicuous."

"Where are you staying?" I later asked Max as we left the club.

"I haven't gotten a place yet."

"You can spend the night in my room. There are two beds."

"Where would that be?"

"In the Starlight Motel down in Jasper."

"That dump?"

"Yeah, it's pretty bad but I wanted to see where Carrie was killed. The owner wouldn't let me see the room unless I paid him a night's fee."

"You mean you're staying in the room where Carrie was killed?"

"Yes and the strangest thing happened there earlier today. I fell asleep and this image floated before me, a beautiful face. She told me to check her theses."

"Do you think Carrie really contacted you?"

"I don't know. I'm open to the possibility.

I do believe in such things."

"Have you ever seen a photo of her?"

"No."

"Sounds like something you should research."

"I intend to. Just follow me," I said as I opened the door to my vehicle."

A short while later Max and I were settled in the small motel room. I chose to retire early but Max pulled a laptop computer from a case and opened it on the small table. He began typing, almost at a frantic pace. "Would you describe again your encounter with the vision of Carrie?"

"Sure." I retold about the milk and honey beauty and the haunting light fragrance that wafted the air as she floated before me. "Are you writing about Carrie?" I asked.

"Yes, you, Carrie, Woody and Shapely; all of you.

I have your permission, don't I? I'm not divulging what Carrie said to you about her thesis. We better keep that to ourselves for now."

"Yes, I said, "If it will help Woody, write all you want."

"Thank you," Max said. The soft tapping of his computer keys lulled me to sleep.

Chapter Fourteen

When I opened my eyes after a sound sleep Max was zipping his bag in preparation to leave. "Hey, you're an early riser. What time is it?"

"Eight."

"Eight o'clock. Gee, I couldn't have slept until eight." I stretched. I didn't want to get up.

Max laughed. "You did, understandable though. We had quite an evening. I was thinking, maybe we ought to warn Shapely about what we discovered. You were right, we can't let her not know and maybe endanger her. How about we meet at the club again tonight and let Shapely know what's going on."

"All right," I replied, relieved that Max had concluded the same as I. "Where are you off to this early?"

He lifted his laptop into a carrying case. "I need to find a connection to the internet. I think the Inn out on the interstate provides the service. I want to get this story out. The Outpost will buy anything I do."

"The Outpost, I've never heard of it."

"It's a small daily in the Philly area, great little press, prints the more intriguing side of the news. It has a huge readership and pays well. What will you do today?"

"I'll probably go sightseeing. The land is so beautiful and wild. What time do you want to meet at the Fantasy Nights?"

"How about eight o'clock, that's when Shapely goes on stage. We'll catch her when she finishes." With a wave of his hand Max was out the door and gone.

Quietness settled around me. I needed to talk to Beth. I imagined her the way she appeared in early morning lying beside me, her hair mussed from sleep. I loved to watch her stretch and wipe the sleep from her eyes. She always turned toward me and smiled when she realized I had been watching her waken.

She should be up and having her morning coffee by now. I quickly dialed her number.

"Hello," she said.

"Hi, Baby," I said as a wave of longing washed over me.

"Hi, Harley, where are you now?"

"I'm in a motel; the place where Carrie was killed."

"Ugh, you can't be serious. Why would you be there?"

"Well . . ." I hesitated. Beth wouldn't understand.

"I'm here as part of my investigation. I . . . I met Shapely last night."

"Who? You met who?" Beth's voice had risen. I imagined her face reddening.

"The exotic dancer who worked with Carrie and I met a reporter, Max . . . something." I had forgotten Max's last name. I was sounding trite, losing my hold on the situation I was in.

"Harley, have you lost your mind? You're a preacher, remember?"

I had forgotten for awhile. "Beth, I think I'm really getting somewhere. I've learned so much. I can't give up now. Two months, that's my sabbatical. That's all I'll take, I promise. I'll stop at the end of two months, no matter what. Okay, Honey?" She hesitated; the line fell silent. "I love you," I said simply.

"All right," she said.

"Two months then we'll get on with our lives; no more prisoners or investigations or anything like that. Right?"

"I promise," I said. Our conversation grew more normal. We discussed the church, our home which we hoped to return to and how we would make amends with the church board. "Everything will work out in the end, Beth. Remember, we walk with God." I hung up and felt better about our relationship.

After a shower and shave I dressed in my other casual pants and shirt. Although the room was mine until twelve o'clock, I had no desire to remain in the room where Carrie had drawn her last breath. "Poor girl," I said aloud.

"Struggling to pay for her education by compromising everything sacred about herself is degrading. God, please forgive her youthful mistakes and give her a home in Heaven."

As I was climbing into my vehicle, my cell phone rang.

Dad was calling. "Hi, Son," the familiar voice greeted me. "How are things going with you?"

"Good, Dad, I think I'm making progress."

"Be careful, Son, you know you're putting yourself in danger. Your Mom's worried sick and so are your brothers and sisters, of course they always wanted to take care of you, you being the youngest."

"I'll be careful, Dad, I promise. Remember Shapely Shaw in the court transcript?"

"Of course." Dad chuckled. "How could I forget? She was an intriguing character."

"I met her and she's nice and I saw Juan Manos and made a friend. His name is Max Holmes, he's a writer."

"Sounds like you're having an interesting experience."

"Yes, more intriguing than I could possibly describe."

"Well, I want you to try. Call me in a couple of days and keep me up to date."

"I will, Dad and tell the family not to worry. Remember God is by my side always."

"Yes and don't forget to ask him to protect you."

"I will, Dad. I love you. Bye."

"Love you too, Son, bye."

I was becoming as one with the hills and hollows of the area as I explored, following dirt roads until they sometimes ended abruptly at the base of a steep incline. I felt I had mastered the art of backing up my vehicle. I found there really was an end of the road. I made another visit to the Market for a hearty lunch and had a short conversation with the motherly lady behind the counter.

In late afternoon I lay my seat back and took a lengthy nap then I finished reading a book I had left forgotten in the car. Finally eight o'clock neared and I headed back to the Fantasy Nights club.

Max was already there, sitting alone in a corner, a half-empty beer bottle on the small table in front of him. He smiled when he saw me.

"Hey, Harley," he called to me. We shook hands which was a habit of mine but which seemed not needed here.

The place was as noisy and smoke-filled as the night before. "I've got some good news," Max exclaimed.

His eyes brightened and he leaned over the table. "My story sold. The Outpost editor loved it and wants more, wants me to stay on the story and report bi- weekly."

"That's great, Max. I guess we need the publicity."

"Yeah, the preacher and the stripper unite to fight for justice, unlikely heroes."

"What? Is . . . is that the angle you presented?" I was in shock. "If my wife sees that, my goose is cooked. I'm already skating on thin ice. Our relationship is hanging by a hair."

Max laughed and slapped me on the shoulder. "Do you have another cliché?"

I laughed too, a bit uncomfortably. "No, at least I hope not, in fact, I don't know where I found those."

"You've been hanging around eastern Kentucky too long. Don't worry; the Outpost is distributed in eastern Pennsylvania. Your wife will never see it."

"Hey Cutie, you're back, here's your free beer." The waitress with the flaming red hair winked at me then came toward me with an exaggerated sway of her hips.

"Thanks, Roxie," I said, feeling a kinship to the buxom redhead with magic in her touch.

"Did I cure that headache?" she asked with a smile as she handed me the bottle of ale..

"Absolutely," I returned and gave her a thumbs up.

A roar of applause drew our attention as the lights came on around the stage and a soft spotlight highlighted Shapely Shaw.

She began gyrating; catching each beat of the rhythmic music.

"She is special, isn't she?" I said as I watched her. I was fascinated by how a woman could capture and use her femininity in such a provocative manner.

"Whoa, preacher, careful, good man," Max warned.

"Oh, I was just admiring her abilities, nothing more." A boundary held my emotions and my actions in check and I would not cross that line.

"Remember why we're here. She may be in danger. We have to warn her."

"Yes." Reluctantly I tore my gaze from the body on stage which seemed to pulse with the roll of drum beats.

"I wonder where she was schooled," Max said. "Looks like dancers I've seen in Rio."

"You've been to South America?" I asked, fascinated. I had been nowhere outside the states.

"Yeah, I'm a writer, remember? I'll chase a story anywhere."

"Then you must be single," I surmised.

"Yes, so far I'm unencumbered, free as the wind."

"I'm married," I said. I didn't remember revealing that information the night before."

"Somehow I knew that, Preacher." He chuckled then changed the subject. "Have you come up with any suspects in Carrie's murder?"

"No, I'm lost I've seen a lot of unsavory characters but a murderer, no."

"Well, right now we've got to think of Shapely's safety. We don't want another murder, especially Shapely. She's a sweet kid, isn't she?"

"Yes," I agreed. "I like her."

"How could such innocence survive in this place?" Max asked then added, "And how long can it last? This atmosphere could destroy the purest of hearts." He looked pointedly at me.

I took note and vowed to remain untouched. Max and I became lost in conversation, plotting where the investigation should take us and speculating where it could.

"Hi, guys." I jerked my head up to see Shapely standing before us. She had changed into a modest blouse over tight blue jeans.

"Hi, Shapely." Max and I greeted her at the same time.

I pulled out a chair and she plopped down, like a youth, dropping the moves of the sexy seductress.

"Anything new?" she asked, her eyes probing Max then me.

"Yes, we discovered something quite important we think."

"Oh? What?"

I checked the crowd around us. "Could we talk in private, maybe in your dressing room?"

"I don't know what's frowned on. Not that they really care, it's just that if any money changes hands (if you know what I mean) they want a cut."

Shapely glanced around. Her eyes settled on the bouncer, Eric Jordan. "He's been watching me closely of late. I don't like him, gives me the creeps.

"Has he tried to hurt you in any way?" I asked, eyeing the burly man with the wide neck and thick arms. I wouldn't want to tangle with the likes of him.

"Oh no, never."

Max spoke up, "Shapely, you go to your dressing room alone. We'll join you when we see the way is clear."

"All right," she answered. "Be careful."

She gave one last uneasy glance toward Eric then rose and left us, heading toward the hall that led to her room.

The bouncer noted her leaving then turned his back to us to attend to other matters in the room.

"Come on, Harley," Max said, rising to his feet. I followed. After a furtive glance, we darted into the men's room. "Good, there's nobody in here."

"Are we going through the loft again?" I asked.

"Yeah, why not? Seems like the best route."

"We might scare Shapely."

"Better us than the murderer."

I nodded my head in agreement. We were more adept this time. Quickly we replaced the ceiling panel behind us and crept across the rafters toward Shapely's room. We listened, making sure she was alone before lifting the panel to the dimly lit space that was her dressing room.

"Hey, Shapely," Max called in a loud whisper. "Don't be scared."

The girl did a quick intake of breath and clasped a hand over her mouth. "What are you doing?" she demanded as we dropped into her room.

"This is why we wanted to talk to you," I said. "We discovered the loft is open across the whole building and . . . and we found a device, a peeping device, aimed into your room and one aimed at the room Carrie used.

Someone has been spying on you. We had to let you know."

"You mean some creep has been looking at me while I change?"

Shapely's face grew pink. A skunk has been getting his jollies by peeping at us. Wait until Mr. Wallace hears about this."

"No, no, Shapely, we don't know who's to blame. It could even be the manager and remember that Carrie was killed. That means this could be the work of the murderer."

Shapely fell into an old stuffed chair. Her fair complexion grew paler. "Oh, for a moment I forgot about Carrie." She glanced up at us with wide frightened eyes. "If the man who murdered Carrie was the one who peeped at her then . . . then I might be next." She clutched a hand about her neck. "He . . . he cut her throat. Oh God, he cut her throat. What am I going to do?"

I could see hysteria building in her. Her breaths were coming in short gasps. We had managed to frighten her terribly. "Don't worry, don't be scared. He may just be a harmless peeping tom. Calm yourself. We'll protect you," I said.

"How? How can you possibly protect me?"

Max and I exchanged a desperate look. Shapely had a point. How could we ever protect her?"

Max spoke up "We'll move in with you, Shapely. We'll be near you at all times till the murderer is captured."

I stared at him in shock, stunned by what he had just said. "Max, are you serious? Move in with Shapely? That's impossible."

"I have two bedrooms, Harley.

You and Max could share one." She wrung her hands. "I'm really scared, first Carrie and now me. He's after me. I'll be the next one killed. Oh, Harley, please help me."

"There must be another way."

I sounded almost as desperate as Shapely.

Max grinned. "Look at it this way, Harley. You're on a sabbatical. You could easily stay a couple of weeks.

I need to follow this story. The Outpost is going to pay me good money. This will be a perfect set up for us and for Shapely."

"But what if the murderer isn't caught?" I argued.

"You mean you're giving up on your quest to free Woody?" Max asked.

"No, of course not . . . but."

"Please, Harley, just for awhile. I'm frightened, really frightened." Shapely wrung her hands.

"If Beth finds out, my marriage could be in trouble."

"Doesn't she trust you, Harley? She should. I trust you," Shapely said.

"All right," I agreed. "But just for a few days."

Within seconds, as if on cue, my cell phone rang. I didn't have to look at the screen, I knew who was calling. I walked away from the pair for a somewhat private conversation.

"Hi, Beth," I tried a deep whisper.

"Harley, is that you?"

"Yes, it's me."

"You sound funny, what's wrong."

"I picked up a little sore throat."

I crossed my fingers behind my back like I did when I was a child. That would cancel out the small lie I had just uttered. "Forgive me, Lord, this is a have- to case."

"Well, if you're having trouble speaking, I'll not keep you. I just wanted to know how you were.

I thought maybe I would drive east one day and visit awhile."

"You, you want to visit me here in eastern Kentucky? Really? But you hate it here."

"I'm willing to overlook the area and people to be with you." Her voice sounded prim and proper as usual.

What would she think of Shapely and Max? I couldn't handle the confrontation. "I don't think that would be a good idea right now.

Give me a few days to get over this throat thing. I wouldn't want you to catch it."

"All right, Harley, if that is the way you want it."

Beth wasn't happy but I didn't know what else to do. "I'll call, Beth, I promise."

"She hung up" I said as I turned toward Max and Shapely.

"Close call, huh, Harley? You'll have time to smooth that out," Max assured me. "You did the right thing. We're too deep in this to back out now."

"You're right," I said. The realization hit me. I had hungered for intrigue and I was wading deeper into it by the hour. Now I understood Dad and his mystery novels. I felt I was writing my own but how was it going to end? A shiver ran up my spine.

"So, Harley, are you with us?" Shapely asked.

"Yes, for now at least."

"Oh, we're kind of like the three musketeers," she squealed. "What do we do now? I'm through for the evening."

"We haven't really made any observations yet. I hate to leave without anything of substance," I said.

"So it's back to the loft," Max stated.

"We'll just sit up there and listen. Maybe we'll get lucky."

"How long?" Shapely asked.

"A couple of hours, I guess," he replied.

Shapely grabbed a pen and a piece of paper.

"Here's directions to my place. I'll be waiting for you," she said.

"Thanks." Max took the note from her hand and stuck it in his pocket.

We scooted the chair in which Shapely had been sitting and used it to ease our climb back into the loft.

"See you guys."

Shapely whispered and gave a light wave of her hand. Her face, gazing up at us was trusting and vulnerable. We had to help her, had to do all we could to protect her, even if that meant moving into her apartment.

We moved about quietly, listening. Soon it began to grow warm in the loft. Vents whirred at each end of the building but the air hardly seemed moved at all. We crept over to where the office was located. Light shone through a tiny crevice in the ceiling. I dropped my head down and peered through the tiny crack.

Mr. Wallace sat at his desk. In front of him huge neat stacks of money covered the desktop.

He would count stacks of bills then jot figures on a pad of paper. He hesitated then picked up a couple of $100's and slipped them into his pocket.

H-m-m-m, I thought. *Mr. Wallace is a bit of a crook, skimming money from the till.* I didn't see how the matter could relate to the case concerning Carrie but I took note and would tell Max later. I couldn't risk the sound of my voice just above where the man sat. I watched as he unlocked a safe where he stored the cash and couldn't help noting the numbers he dialed although I had no interest in the combination.

Three loud distinct raps sounded at his door. Mr. Wallace jumped up and hurriedly turned the lock to allow entry. The man looked familiar. Yes, he was one of the goons at Juan Manos's back, unattractive, in fact, quite ugly with thick features and a squat figure.

"Come . . . . come in, Carlos," the manager stammered.

"Manos wants his take tonight," was all the man said with a thick Latino accent. He placed a briefcase on the desk.

"But Manos usually gets paid on Saturday night."

"Yes, but he is leaving town. He needs money now."

"Well, all right, but I'll have to make note. This will throw my books off." The manager hurried back to the safe and twisted the dial. "Are you sure this is what Manos wants?"

"You not trust Carlos?" The man leaned on the desk and peered over it, reminding me of an ape. Mr. Wallace frantically turned the dial.

"Oh no, I know how close the two of you are. It's just unusual, you know." He grabbed a bag and stuffed it full of bills, the ones of large denominations. He handed it to the man who crammed it inside the briefcase. "Here, sign this," he said, handing the man his book.

The man did as he was told then clutching the thick black bag he left the room.

Max and I scooted away from the area. I whispered to him what I had witnessed.

"Well, we know the manager is skimming money and we also know Manos has some element of control over the club. Not much but something to go on."

"Since Manos is leaving the club we may as well leave too," Max added.

We crawled back to where we usually exited the loft.

"S-h-h-h-h," Max whispered. "Someone's in the men's room." We waited quietly until the way would be clear.

Two males mumbled below us. One raised his voice "Ed, please, you got to share, man. I got to have a fix now, just enough till Saturday. We're friends, man. Eric said Manos will be burning off a big batch, and it'll be ready then."

"Hell, I might not have enough for myself if I go giving it to you,"

"I heard you could cut it with weed.

You'll never know the difference in the high; just sprinkle the crack over the weed. You'll get a longer burn"

"Okay," the other agreed. "But you owe me, man."

"Thanks, man. Don't worry, I pay my debts." With a sigh of thankfulness from one man they left the room.

Max and I shared shocked expressions. I held my breath then let out a long sigh.

We listened to a moment of stillness before dropping into the room. "Wow, what are we getting into?" Max breathed a deep breath.

"Murder, drugs, peeping toms, what next?" He rubbed a hand over his brow as if to question his sanity.

I didn't answer. I couldn't, just managed a helpless shrug of my shoulders. I was sure thankful for his help. I would never have made it alone.

Max dug in his pocket for the scrap of paper with Shapely's address. "Let's go . . . home."

Shapely lived in an apartment building appearing to be about four units.

Thankfully the parking lot was large enough to accompany our extra vehicles.

She opened the door immediately to our knock. "Come in and just make yourselves at home," she said with that easy Eastern

Kentucky way. "Your bedroom is in there." She pointed. Her face was washed of makeup and she was dressed in a modest housecoat over modest pajamas. She could have been your average girl next door.

"Wow, what an evening," I said as I dropped into a chair.

"What happened?" Shapely asked. "You want a cup of coffee? I just made some."

"Sure, thanks," I replied. A cup of coffee was just what I needed.

"Me too," Max called from the small room we had been assigned.

I took my steaming brew and sat down on the sofa. Shapely sat in a chair opposite and leaned forward in anticipation of what I would tell.

"While we were in the loft I found a place to peek into the manager's office.

I saw him take money from the funds he was counting, looked like a couple of hundred."

"I never really trusted him but then he has a sick wife and a lot of medical expenses."

Shapely's understanding of Mr. Wallace's actions didn't surprise me. Max was right, she was a sweet kid. I hurried on.

"One of Manos' men came to the office and demanded money for his boss- a large amount too."

"I knew the pig had . . ."

Shapely stopped abruptly and slapped her hand over her mouth. "I'm sorry, that's what all the girls call the man, I mean Mr. Manos. I knew he had some control over the club but I didn't know why."

Max walked back into the room and added. "That's not all; there were two guys in the men's room sharing drugs. They had gotten the stuff from Eric who was selling it for Manos. Another shipment is due in on Saturday according to those two."

"Oh my gosh." Shapely fell back in her chair, obviously shocked.

"Did you have any idea this was going on?" Max directed his question to Shapely.

"No, no, I had no idea. I perform. I'm a dancer. I do my job and then leave. I don't work the floor like the other girls. I'm special; I'm hands off. I'm supposed to turn the guys on, you know. I'm the unattainable, Mr. Wallace says. The other girls benefit from my teasing.

They get the extra money; I just get my pay, which is pretty good. Mr. Wallace says I'm worth it."

"You're definitely a good dancer," Max and I agreed. She smiled.

My mind strayed to Carrie Ann. I had to know. "What about Carrie (Lola)? Was she special too?"

Shapely's expression fell, visibly saddened. "She was special . . . but." She hesitated.

"But what?" Max seemed just as interested as I.

"Well, Carrie was beautiful, I mean really beautiful. She had long curly blondish red hair." Shapely lifted her hands around her head and over her shoulders, as if visualizing her.

I was reminded of the vision in the motel. Shapely seemed to be describing what I saw.

Had I really been visited by Carrie's spirit? I was getting more motivated, yet a little nervous.

"And she was curvy, I mean really curvy. She had brains; was going to college and all that kind of stuff." She hesitated and sighed.

Max and I urged her to continue. This was really important. "Well, you know it's not nice to speak ill of the dead but I guess you need to know everything.

"She was kind of close to the pig." She had let the derogatory word slip. "He liked her better than everybody else. All the men did. She made lots of money I'm sure. Woody wasn't always around. He didn't see everything. She worked the floor like the other girls and she'd get felt up a lot.

There's a private room in the back. You have to go through the storage area. I don't know what goes on in that room. I didn't want to know but Carrie knew. She went there lots of times if a guy had enough money.

Manos had the money I heard it referred to as the getting off room."

Shapely fell silent and so did we then she added, "I think Carrie needed lots of money for her schooling and things. She wanted to be a doctor of something weird to take care of crazy people. Strange," she continued, "I'm just an ordinary country girl but I think what she was doing was 'crazy'."

Max and I sat sipping our coffee. What could we say?

I think we were both digesting the facts of Carrie Ann's life.

Medical school was expensive but to go to such lengths. The money couldn't have been easy. Max broke the silence.

"Poor girl."

You know this opens up a whole slew of possible suspects. How many men had she come in contact with? How can we ever sort through them all?"

With a sigh he reached for his laptop. "Shapely, do you have a photo of Carrie Ann?"

"Yes," she replied. "I have her publicity photos. They were taken by a professional photographer. She was very proud of them." She rushed into her bedroom to retrieve the pictures.

My heart jumped. I would see the girl of whom I had been imagining. Shapely returned to the room clutching a folder. She handed it to Max. I peeked over his shoulder. There was the girl of my vision, a stunning, beautiful girl, almost breathtaking.

Max whistled. "No wonder she was so popular. Time for a new installment. Oh, don't worry." He glanced toward me.

I won't reveal about Carrie's tie to the room. She's just a young girl trying to get through medical school."

"Thanks, Max," I said.

"Yes, thank you on Carrie's behalf," Shapely added.

That night in dream, I found myself in a barroom, small with a low ceiling. The place was dimly lit with at least a hundred people. Red velvet encased the oval bar and covered the tops of stools. Smoke thickened the air.

Shrill female voices pierced the den of noise. The people about were caricatures, females with overly painted faces and men with round protruding bellies and red jowls hanging from their faces, all in assorted stages of drunkenness. Their laughter mocked me; you don't belong here, get out, get out, you are not one of us. I rushed for the door; it was heavy, I struggled to push it open. The loud mass behind me was closing in. I awoke in a sweat, my heart pounding. I wiped my eyes to rid myself of the nightmare. Max lay sleeping peacefully on his side of the bed.

The next morning Max was whistling. He had gotten up early and gone to the local McDonalds for coffee and sandwiches. His laptop was open on the table.

Shapely rose about the same time as I. "I could have made breakfast," she said.

"I needed Wi-Fi anyway," he said, grinning. "Eat your breakfast; I have a surprise for you."

"A surprise?" Shapely's voice lifted.

"Yeah, I hope you both like it."

For some reason my stomach felt uncomfortable. I was afraid I knew what the surprise would be and that I wouldn't like it. The coffee and sandwich made me feel better.

When we had finished, Shapely said, "Now, show us the surprise."

"Okay," Max said. "Close your eyes."

We were sitting around a small table. I heard Max moving his PC. "All right, open your eyes," he said.

There on the screen was the image of a newspaper story. The picture he had snapped of Shapely and me sitting at a table in the club jumped out at me.

Everyone would see my image, Reverend Harley Danials with a big-busted blond with painted eyes and lips. *Preacher and Stripper fight to free prisoner on death row.*

"Oh, I'm in the news. That's a great picture, Max," Shapely gushed.

My eyes quickly scanned the story relating my conviction that Woodrow Howard Pierce was innocent and was on a quest with the help of club stripper, Shapely Shaw to prove his innocence.

"What do you think?" Max asked, his voice filled with pride.

Shapely laughed and clapped her hands. "It's wonderful, Max. I always wanted to be famous. I just didn't consider the unusual route that I would be taking. Fate is as unpredictable as the weather."

"Harley?" Max questioned my silence.

"I guess we need the publicity. Are . . . are you sure this is just in Pennsylvania?"

"Yeah, small press, I promise. Beth won't see it. That's a long way from Kentucky." He laughed. "You're safe, Preacher."

"Safe?" I asked.

"Well, maybe that was the wrong word to use." He chuckled.

"Just think – first Pennsylvania then the whole country then Hollywood." Shapely had stars in her eyes.

"Whoa," I said. "Shapely, this can't get out right now.

Remember we're doing a murder investigation and drugs are involved. Our cover can't be blown until this thing is done."

"You mean I can't even show this to my mother?"

"No, not yet, maybe later. Right Max?"

"Yeah, right, maybe later." Max seemed a little uncomfortable.

Chapter Fifteen

That afternoon we were sitting around discussing all the elements of our predicament."I wonder who the peeper is." Shapely asked. "I have thought and thought and can't imagine anyone I know doing such a thing."

"I wish there was some way to flush him out," I said.

Max rubbed his chin thoughtfully. "There might be a way to do that."

"Oh? How?"

"Yes, how?" Shapely added.

"Tease him, entice him, put the urge in him."

"How could he possibly be more teased, that's my job, that's what I do," she said, with a flip of her hair.

"I was thinking, maybe if you get on the floor and mix with the crowd, maybe get closer to him . . . uh . . . arouse him sorta."

"Max," I responded, shocked, "that's asking a lot of Shapely. Do you think that would really be worthwhile?"

"I'm not sure of anything at this point. I don't think any of us are. It was just a suggestion."

"I don't mind," Shapely said.

"I'll just do it once though. If it will help Woody, besides I want to know who that creep is anyway."

"Tonight might be the best time," Max said..

" It's Friday so the place will be packed. All the regulars will be there."

Just what am I supposed to do?" she asked, with a doubtful expression.

"Not much, just walk around, smile, say hello, let them be near enough to smell your fragrance. Evidently the guy is enamored with you," Max said.

"But what about Carrie? Was the man enamored with her too?" I asked. I wasn't comfortable with how we were using Shapely. I felt we were playing with fire.

"I'm not a criminologist, maybe Carrie first and now that she is gone he turned his attention to Shapely. We're all feeling our way here."

"You're right," I conceded. Suddenly I had a strong urge to pray. "Do you mind if we take it to the Lord?"

"Please do," Shapely said with a smile. "I was raised a Baptist, you know."

"A Baptist?" I asked. With her line of work I assumed she had not had God in her life.

"So, I strayed from the way a little but I do have my standards."

"I'm sure you do," I replied.

I reached out and clasped a hand of each of my friends.

"Dear Lord, we're about to put Shapely in a position in which she isn't comfortable. Be with her, Lord. This is all done to procure the freedom of an innocent man. Please guide each of us and keep us safe in our endeavor. Thank you for your protection and guidance. We are in need of your divine power. This I pray in Jesus' name, Amen."

"Amen," Shapely added emphatically.

"I never was a praying man," Max said with a grin, but I figure we need all the help we can get."

Friday evening came all too quickly. Before Shapely left for work, I asked Max, "After Shapely mixes with the crowd, how are we going to know if someone goes to the loft. No one would ever do such a thing if we were in the men's room."

"I've been thinking about that and here's what I came up with. Shapely sat down to hear Max's scheme. "There are five stalls in there, okay. I made an 'out of order' sign and I'll tape it to the door of one and latch it from inside, then I hide by sitting on the tank with my feet on the lid of the john.

No one will suspect I'm in there.

If I'm right, the guy will be excited by the closeness of his idol and want to . . . uh. . get a better look."

"Let's hope he doesn't choose the stall right next to you or he might look down and see you," I said.

"You know, when we went up, the end panel seemed loose.

That's why I came up with the idea, so let's just hope that's the one he uses."

"But I don't want this pervert to see me completely naked. I know I expose my breasts on stage. In some strange way, because they're implants, I feel they're not really me. They're just things like makeup that I need for my career." She lowered her gaze. "I guess that doesn't make sense."

I didn't have an answer. Her logic didn't make sense to me.

"I understand," Max said to her with a gentle smile which she returned.

"Sometimes life pushes us down a path and it's hard to turn around so in our minds we compromise."

"I made a mental note to try to be more understanding. I recalled the adage, not to judge a person until you walked a mile in his shoes.

"What do I do if this guy acts? Do I stop him?" I asked.

"No, no, let's just try to find out who he is then I'll do a background check. We don't want a confrontation yet."

"Okay, so I'll just wait and keep an eye on the others in the room.

Since it is Friday there may be some new faces in the crowd."

"Yes, a lot of faces. Fridays are packed," Shapely added.

"So we have a plan. Let's hope something happens." Max lay his hand atop Shapely's hand that lay on the table. I added mine.

We were partners. We would have each other's back. We didn't have to say the words.

The evening stretched slowly. Max and I entered the club just before Shapely ended her act. She had been right; the place was full to capacity and noisy. I could hardly hear Max but I understood his signal that he was headed for the men's room.

I nursed my beer and scooted to a spot where I could watch the ones who entered the men's room. Several made the trip, some two or three at a time.

They had obviously consumed a lot of drink but they all exited and joined the throng on the floor. Then Eric Jordan worked his way across the floor. Something about his manner, the way he checked around him as if to see if he were being watched.

I turned my back to him just as he glanced my way. I returned my gaze just as he entered the restroom. I waited and he didn't exit. I checked my watch to time him.

I was puzzled. Eric was a tall muscular man. I assumed he could get any woman he desired.

What if he only wanted the unattainable? What urge would make him resort to such a despicable act? Could there ever be an explanation for such behavior? Finally, after twenty minutes, he emerged. I checked him closely. He appeared much the same except he had a smile on his face. I turned my back to him as he reentered the room.

I rushed to find Max. I had to know. Max was exiting the locked stall as I entered.

"We have our man," he said. "At least we have our peeping tom. That doesn't mean he's also the murderer."

"No, but at least we have a suspect. We've got to tell Shapely."

"You hang around in here," Max said. "I'll make a quick trip to the panel over her room and let her know the mission is complete." He quickly hoisted himself into the loft then reappeared seconds later.

He gave me a thumb's up sign.

"We can leave now, Shapely will be out soon."

Outside we waited. Soon the girl appeared. She clutched her arms around herself in a protective manner. "I can't believe it. Eric!

I always felt he was a brute of a man and I never liked him but to do what he is doing. I'm shocked. I mean there are naked girls all over the place and most of them are easy."

Shapely shook her head in disbelief. "Do you think he is the killer?" Her gaze searched first Max then me.

"We don't know, Shapely," I said.

"What will we do next?" she asked.

Max rubbed his chin. "Let us think about it. We'll come up with something. There has to be a logical second step and we'll find it somehow."

Chapter Sixteen

The next step came soon, a shock to me; in fact it rocked my world. Max had submitted the next installment of his story. That morning he came back clutching his laptop to his chest. A look of wonderment was on his face. He sat down and stared into space.

"Max," I said, "what's happened? Are you all right?"

Finally, his eyes flicked up to me. "I don't know how to tell you this."

"Tell me what?" My heart started beating faster at his hesitation. "I've got to know."

"Our story has been picked up by Associated Press."

"I know nothing about newspapers; what does that mean?"

"It means my story will be all over the country . . .everywhere!"

Sweat popped out on my brow. My weak body dropped into a chair. "The picture?" I asked. "The one with Shapely and me?"

"Pictures," Max corrected.

"But you told me only in Pennsylvania, nowhere else."

"How was I to know?" Max seemed as surprises as I. "The story caught on. They want more, more details, more pictures, bios on Woody and you and Shapely."

Max's voice rose with excitement. "This could be big, Harley. This could be my ticket."

"Yes, it could be mine too, a ticket to nowhere. I'll be ruined. The church will never take me back, and Beth, oh God, Beth." I couldn't go further. What had I done?

"There's one good point, the publicity will be good for Woody's case. Maybe the court system will pay attention and give it a second look"

"Yes, but someone else will be made aware of what we're doing also, the real murderer. If we start getting close to the truth, we could all be in danger. This could lead to real trouble, Max."

"Look Preacher, you prayed for help and guidance, maybe this is that aid. I had no idea this would happen, it's like fate. We're just going to have to deal with it."

"Deal with what?" Shapely strolled into the room, stifling a yawn.

"You wanted to be famous, well, I'm afraid your dream is about to become a reality," I said."Tell her, Max."

Max glanced at me then took a deep breath.

"Our story is going to be read all over the nation. It's been picked up."

"Oh Max, is this for real?"

At Max's affirmative nod, she rushed and threw her arms around his neck, squealing as she went. Suddenly she sobered.

"What will they say at the club? What will Mr. Wallace do? I may be fired when he finds out."

"We've really stirred up a bee's nest with this story, Max." I said. How can we work undercover? The management, the peeper, drug dealers, the murderer, not to mention my wife; they all will know. Our investigation just hit a brick wall."

I paced the floor before Max and Shapely. Max chuckled.

"What's so funny?" I demanded.

"You and your sayings; I swear, Preacher, you're becoming a hillbilly at a record pace."

I did see the humor in my words and we all shared a laugh. At least the tension was relieved and I did stop my pacing.

"Who knows, maybe this is the way. We'll have to roll with the punches." I caught myself and we all laughed again. "Max, please edit my speech in your story."

"All right, let's get down to business," Max said. "I need more info on Woody, Harley."

"I'll call my father and have him fax records to the local library."

"Do you have a picture of the Eddyville prison? This angle about it being called a castle is interesting."

"I can easily get one," I responded.

"Good, this next installment should get some attention. We're all going to be famous."

Boy, were Max's words prophetic. Little did we know what was about to erupt. It all began that evening when we entered the club at the usual time, as Shapely went on stage.

Before, no one noticed us, just a couple of guys in the crowd. That night everyone seemed to be sneaking furtive glances our way. When Shapely appeared on stage for her act, a hush fell over the rowdy crowd. As she performed, all eyes watched. I have always heard that news traveled fast, now I understood just how fast. Shapely seemed a little stiff in her performance, still great, but maybe a little pre-occupied. As she neared the end of her performance, Eric, the bouncer, worked his way through the throng toward Max and me. He and I exchanged uneasy glances.

"Are you Max and Harley?" he asked in a gruff loud voice.

"Yes, that's our names," I replied in a steady voice although my insides quaked.

"Come with me," he commanded.

"Wait a minute," Max objected, "Just where are you taking us?" A couple of tough-looking guys stepped out of the crowd to our backs. They were Hispanic – Manos' men.

One of them prodded Max in the back. "Okay, okay," Max said, tugging his jacket away from the man's thick fingers. We followed meekly behind Eric, through the crowd, down the hallway and into the office in which we had peered from above.

In the room stood Shapely, still in her stage attire of thin silver tendrils and spike silver heels. Her face was pale and frightened.

Her lips were trembling. I wanted to comfort her but dared not make such a move.

In a chair sat Mr. Wallace and behind the desk was Manos himself. He reared back in the chair and eyed the two of us. His dark face was unreadable. At least I did not see anger.

"I hear we got us a trio of private eyes investigating this club," Manos said in a deep voice void of emotion. His eyes though, burned with unwavering intense curiosity.

"We . . . we're looking into Carrie Ann's death and since she worked here." Max wasn't allowed to finish.

"Lola," Manos said, interrupting Max. He sighed and his face softened for a moment. "She was special." His voice hardened again. "There are things about this club that are off limits, you hear? The regular business is open to you but me and my people don't exist. Do you get that, punks?

We don't exist. My name nor any of my people will not be mentioned in your story." He put emphasis on the repeated words.

"Yes, yes, we understand," I said. All the while I thought, you are the club.

"Strictly a male-entertainment establishment," Manos continued. I think you could refer to it as a gentleman's club.

Do I make myself clear?"

"Yes," Max and I agreed.

"Which one of you gentlemen is the writer?" he asked in a more normal tone.

"I am the writer," Max said. I marveled at his coolness.

"Not a word. I think we understand one another, right?

Manos stared into Max's eyes reaffirming his words. "Yes I understand perfectly, not a word, not a hint," Max replied.

"Have a seat," he said to the two of us. He motioned to a couple of chairs in front of the desk. He leaned forward, folding his arms. He wore a black silk shirt and heavy cologne. The air felt heavy, dark and foreboding. "You know, I've been waiting for you to show up."

Neither Max nor I replied but I'm sure our faces revealed our shock and surprise. What was he talking about. Why would he be waiting for us?

"I mean somebody to find out what happened to my girl, my Lola. I want to know. I never believed that Woody boy did it, but the damned police wouldn't look any farther. Bunch of hicks couldn't see beyond their damn noses.

Being who I am (in my questionable position) I couldn't come forward with questions. Me and the damn police don't mix."

I gasped a deep breath. I had the sense of drowning. Here I was, sitting in a darkened back room conversing with an obvious drug kingpin. The situation took on a surreal feeling. Had I lost my mind?

"I want to know what you've found out so far. Do you have any suspicions, any suspects?" His manner demanded an answer.

"We've really just began our investigation," I said. "So far we have no suspects."

Manos stared at me with hard probing black eyes. He wasn't satisfied with my answer. What more could I say.

I quickly searched my mind. "I compiled a list of people that I found suspicious after reading the trial transcript. I can tell you who we've eliminated."

"Do you have that list with you?" he asked simply yet in a gruff voice.

"Yes, I carry it in my pocket."

"Let me see it," he demanded, holding out a wide hand.

I hesitated. "Give it to him, Harley," Max said urgently. He had lost his coolness. Manos scared him. I pulled out the folded paper and handed it to the man.

His eyes scanned the list. "Shapely?" He asked incredibly.

"Her name is crossed out of course." I said apologetically.

Shapely gasped. "You thought I . . ." She clasped her hand over her mouth in shock.

"I'm sorry, that was before I met you, Shapely. I marked you off immediately." She smiled, seeming relieved.

Manos reached for an ink pen. "My name is on here. I'll do the honors if you don't mind." He used a black marker and covered his name completely. "That's one less suspect. Who is Mr. Adkins ?" he asked.

"He is the man who owns the motel where Carrie Ann was killed."

"You eliminated him!"

"Yes, he was old and weak. He could have never overpowered Carrie."

"This is a short list.

There are hundreds of men who frequent this joint and knew Carrie." Manos's voice held skepticism.

"But she opened the door willingly. There was no forced entry so I figured she knew the person well," I answered, explaining my rationale.

"Makes sense." Manos nodded his head. He scanned the remaining names on my list then glanced at each figure in the room. His eyes rested on Eric, who squirmed uncomfortably under his scrutiny. The club manager nervously averted his gaze.

"I'm adding a couple of names on here," he said as he scratched on my paper with a pen. "What else do you know?" he asked. His gaze raked me and then Max.

Max spoke up. "So far I'm just writing background stuff.

I'm letting the readers get acquainted with Woody, the Preacher and Shapely. I did mention the Fantasy Nights Club which will give it a sizable amount of publicity." Max waited, checking how Manos would react.

"That means it could get busier around here. Maybe we'll move that back wall; use more of the storage area. We could add another two thousand square feet to the floor. Get on that Wallace." he said to the manager." He turned toward Shapely. "How do you fit into this scheme, girl?"

Shapely's voice trembled. "I think I'm kinda the bait for the killer, first Carrie then maybe me." She hurried on.

"I volunteered. I wanted to help Woody because I testified at his trial and I think I unknowingly helped the prosecution. We're kind of like the three musketeers."

She used the childish breathless voice that was her persona. Manos sat rubbing the stubble on his round chin.

"I've got one condition you have to agree too," he said, "before I allow you to go any further." He lowered his hand and balled it into a fist.

My heart was thumping so loudly it seemed others must hear. "What is the condition?" Max asked.

"When you find the guilty dog you turn him over to me."

"But ," I began. He held up his hand to hush me.

I was overwhelmed. "I couldn't do such a thing. What about justice? The court? The law?" Max cleared his throat..

"Look what they've done so far! Justice? I will dispense the justice for my little Lola.

I and only I will wield her murderer's punishment. I have no use for the damn courts."

"But what about Woody? We're trying to free an innocent man too," I said.

"Don't worry, you find me my man and Woody will be freed." He lowered his voice which raged with pent up fury. You do not ask me how or why or when? You ask me none of these things. Is that clear?"

Max and I stared into each other's eyes for a long moment then we dropped our heads in submission. I did whisper under my breath, "Lord, thy will be done, please."

"You want to see my Carrie's room? I've kept it locked since she was killed. Like I said, I've been waiting for you. Maybe you find evidence."

"Yes, we would like to see her room," Max said.

We followed quietly behind the stocky short figure as he marched down the hallway. He lifted a ring and retrieved a small key to loosen the padlock.

We entered almost reverently. Her clothes were still scattered about the room. Her makeup spilled over the top of a dressing table.

I caught my breath for on the wall was a poster of a stunning beauty – Carrie in a relaxed, natural, smiling pose. I knew her for I had seen her before in Shapely's photo, and in the vision I had while staying at the motel. Her spirit had really reached out to me.

I pointed, drawing Max's attention to the photo.

He did a quick intake of breath. "May I take a picture of her likeness?" he asked Manos.

"Yes you may," he returned. "I want the world to see her beauty. I want them to grieve for her. I want them to know my lovely Lola." He kissed his fingers and touch them to her likeness. Could a fiend like him really feel love I wondered. Max snapped his camera several times. Manos continued rubbing his hand over her likeness.

We searched the room, rummaging through drawers, peering under a settee and searching the pockets of her clothing. "Did the police search the room?" Max asked.

"Yes, but it was a damn farce. They already had their man," Manos grumbled.

"I think I've found something," Max said as he withdrew a folded piece of paper from a zipped pocket of a leather jacket. "Just one word, might mean something.

Actually it isn't a word, just some letters – secficb."

"What could that mean?" I asked.

"Who knows?" Max replied. "Keep it though, might be important." He handed the piece of paper to me.

When our search was complete, we quietly left the room. I had the odd sensation that I had just been to a funeral, a sad goodbye to the remains of a life.

"I think we're through for the night," I said. I had to get away from the distasteful man whose hand I was shaking. I needed to think about the agreement we had just made. I rubbed my hand down my side.

It burned from his touch or my imagination. I had just made a deal with the devil or one of his servants. We three climbed into my vehicle. Shapely was too shaken to drive.

"We are in deep shit," Max groaned. "Please excuse my language."

"What are we going to do?" Shapely asked, almost in tears.

"I honestly don't know," Max said."Let's go home and sleep on it. Maybe tomorrow we'll have clearer heads."

Who could sleep? I thought. What a mess. I had only meant to help Woody. It seemed I had started a war, an underworld war. "May God be with us."

Chapter Seventeen

Max was busy pounding his keyboard the next morning. I picked up my cell phone and disconnected the charger. It would be a busy instrument today for sure. I would call Beth, my father and maybe a call to Howard would also be a good idea.

The situation had spun out of our control. I felt like I was being washed out to sea by a huge wave. Land and safety was a distant blur. No one was around to rescue me, throw me a lifeline.

As I was about to dial Dad, the phone rang in my hand. I sat down before answering. It was my father.

"Harley," he said. "I read about you in our newspaper. Wow, I can't believe it, my son, the preacher." An excited laugh burst from my father. "I bet this is the most exciting time of your life.

"Boy, how I'd like to be there with you, Harley, and work with you but Mom wouldn't stand for it. That Shapely is a beauty. The two of you sure make a pair. Everybody I see makes a comment. I've been following your story in the paper. It's almost like reading a mystery novel only bit by bit. There was even a discussion on the local television station, you being a local boy. Max is a good writer.

Is there anything I can do to help? Huh?"

I realized I had not said one word except 'Hello'.

Dad was all wrapped up in (my adventure). "Yes Dad, there is.

Could you fax a copy of the trial transcript to the library here? Max wants to take a look at it. I'll call you the number."

"I'll get that to you today, anything to help. This is so exciting. I feel like you're living one of those books I read. Tell me what you've been doing so far." I recounted the last few days for him, all except Manos of course. "Throw in a peeping tom!" Dad exclaimed.

"Yes, can you believe it?"

"Don't get in over your head, Son." My dad finally thought to caution me.

"I'm not in over my head, I'm just about up to my neck," I replied with a chuckle.

"Well, remember David in the lion's den. God took care of him."

"Yes," I said, as warmth enveloped me. "I'm sure He is with me."

We hung up moments later. Now, it was time to call Beth. I drew a deep breath as I punched her number sequence. Her phone rang and rang and rang. I knew my name would appear on her screen. She knew the call was from me. Her voice mail came on. I couldn't leave a message.

I needed to talk to her personally. A message would have seemed cold. Oh Beth, what have I done to you?

I sat holding the phone in my hand. When it rang, I jumped, nearly dropping the instrument. She was calling me back, but it wasn't her. Howard was calling.

He had been next on my list. "Hello, Howard," I said.

"Hey, Harley, how are you doing up there in West Virginia? Stirring up enough trouble?" He laughed.

"More than you could possibly know, Howard."

"I just wanted you to know I can cover your back if you need. I carry a snub nose .38 and it's legal. I took my training. I can cut the whiskers off a cat at forty yards".

"A gun! Oh no, Howard, no guns." What was happening? I began to doubt everything about myself. Had I, without my knowledge, let evil into my life? Was I really doing the Lord's work?

"Summer told me to thank you, Shapely and the writer who's doing the stories in the newspapers. You should have seen her face, Harley. She has hope. She had given up, you know. She thinks you'll really secure Woody's freedom. Oh, and she said she'd pray every night for your safety."

I had my answer immediately. I would not doubt myself again. "I still think a little added protection would be a good idea. You know I can come up there and help. My guys can keep this place going without me."

"Thanks Howard but we're okay for now. I would appreciate a photo of Woody e-mailed to Max today." I gave him the address and waited while he jotted it down.

" We have eliminated a couple of suspects. I guess that's all we can do for now. Eventually our list will hold fewer names."

"The process of elimination," Howard said. "That makes sense. Well, keep me posted, Preacher."

"I will, Howard and thanks for everything."

Howard's words rang in my ears, 'the process of elimination.' I pulled out my list of suspects. Manos had added a couple of names. I checked them. One was Carlos Garcia and the other was Alfonzo Cortez, both evidently were Hispanic.

I ran them over in my mind. Carlos Garcia rang a bell.

Shapely had mentioned him. Yes, I remembered- he was the man in the office with the briefcase collecting Manos' money. On the other I drew a blank, probably another of his men.

Max interrupted my thoughts. "What about that trial transcript, Harley? I need it today."

"I'll have it for you and a photo of Woody too. You should be getting that soon."

"So." Max hesitated. Let's just take one day at a time.

I've got my angle for today and I'll use the picture of Woody. Tomorrow I'll work on the trial transcript."

"Max, this is more than a story." I was growing a little irritated.

My friend was losing perspective. "People's lives are at stake here."

"I know that, Harley, but this is my part. This is what I do and I think it will bring results. All right?" Max seemed a little stressed too.

"Yes," I said. "I'm sorry, I'll get the transcript today at the library, and hopefully continue this process of elimination." Howard's words were hanging in my brain.

Max's eyes brightened. "That's great, Harley. That will be my next angle - the process of elimination."

Our eyes locked.

"We're all doing the best we can." He shrugged his shoulders.

"Yesterday we had no idea what we would do. One day at a time, Preacher, we'll get there."

He turned and thoughtfully scratched his head.

"It's almost like we're being led. I believe we're going to free Woody."

Shapely walked into the room. She had not yet groomed her hair. It was all mussed like a child's. Her arms were folded tightly. "I'm scared, guys. Manos means business. We'll have to be more careful now that he's involved."

"Don't be frightened." I tried to reassure her and myself. "We'll be with you all the time. We won't ask you to do anything else that might endanger you."

She smiled hesitantly. Her gaze dropped to the list of names I had laid on the coffee table. She picked it up.

"Those two names that Manos wrote in; do you know either of those men?"

"Oh yes," she replied easily.

"Carlos is Manos's right hand man. He does everything for him, is always at his side."

The man I saw carrying the briefcase and picking up the money for Manos, perhaps?"

"Was he overweight and ugly?" she asked.

"Yes," I said, recalling the wide face with hanging jowls, squat nose and receding hairline.

"Unfortunately for him, because of his appearance none of the girls want to be near him.

Even his money won't compensate and he knows it, and Alfonzo is a bodyguard, always with Manos, usually stands at his back. Before Manos enters a room Alfonzo goes in first and inspects the place then brings him in."

I recalled the burly man standing behind Manos while he sat at a table with the dancer atop. He stood like a lion guarding his kill. I shuttered. I had never known such unsavory characters existed outside the movie screen.

Max tapped his last key with a loud, "Yes, this is good."

"At least one of us is positive," Shapely said, dropping her head into her hands as she rested her elbows on the table.

I had to be cheerful no matter what I was feeling. I had to brighten Shapely's face. "So, it's Saturday, what are the plans for the day?" I asked the two.

"I really need to pick up my car. I don't like leaving it in the lot at the club," Shapely said. " Harley, will you escort me to visit my mother, today? I really am uneasy about being alone."

"Sure, after I visit the library and receive the fax my father is sending."

Max joined in, "I'll get my story in. I got the picture of Woody from Howard. He looks like a cool guy, which is good. He has an appealing face.

Once I get the transcript, I'll pour over it, so my day will be full."

"I checked my watch. The library would be open. I could go for the faxes while Shapely showered and readied herself.

Later I sat at a table loading paper for the faxes that were pouring in (to the chagrin of the librarian). "How many papers you are you printing there?

"That's going to be expensive," she warned me. Her eyes peered at me over dark-rimmed reading glasses. She looked the part with her hair severely pulled back into a chignon.

I straightened my pile of papers like a child caught being naughty. Eventually I had my transcript. Thankfully Dad had left out the mundane rituals of the court. I walked up to the counter to pay the usage fee.

"That will be one hundred twenty-five dollars," the stern-faced lady said.

I repeated her. The fee seemed quite high.

"Do you realize how much ink you used? That stuff is expensive."

"Of course, will you take a check?"

She stared at me with a cool gaze. "What's the number on your check?"

I quickly looked.

"It's 5806, an old account. I've had it for years."

"All right," she said.

"I jotted in the amount, handed it to the lady then picked up my load of papers and headed for the door, glad to get away from the dour glare of the old biddy. "Oh, forgive me. Lord I know she's your child too."

I dropped the load of papers on the sofa beside Max. "Trial transcript," I said simply.

"Thanks, Harley, this will help more than you can imagine."

"It had better. I had to face down a tiger to get it."

"What?" Max asked with a puzzled expression.

"Never mind. You wouldn't understand."

Shapely walked in with her purse hanging from her shoulder. "I'm ready to go."

"How about I drive you to your mother's house? Your car has already sat in the club lot overnight. It should be safe during the light of day then you can drive it home after your performance tonight. Max and I will follow."

"That makes sense," she agreed. I opened the door and she climbed into my vehicle. "I think you'll like my mom.

She divorced my father when I was about five or six years old. He moved away. I still have his picture though."

"Have you never had a relationship with your father?"

"No, he remarried. He and my mom never got along so he just made a new life for himself."

She directed me from one winding road onto another.

I was struck anew by the lush beauty of the countryside.

Scenic fence rows wound around and over the hills. Creeks cut jagged paths through the hollows.

As we plunged down a particularly steep mountain, dropping deeper and deeper into a hollow, I had the impression of a roller coaster after a steep final descent.

After we crossed a bridge at the bottom of the ravine the road seemed to rise up the other side at a very steep angle. Could we actually drive upward at such a degree? I visualized my SUV tipping backward and rolling end over end.

"This place is called Sinking Creek," she said matter-of-factly.

"I can see why. That's an awfully steep incline ahead." I tried to quell the unease in my voice as my vehicle climbed up the roller coaster hill.

"Oh, it's nothing." She laughed. "Except in the winter when snow or ice is on the ground. Folks around here know to stock up on supplies like food and fuel. This hollow is so deep the road won't clear off even if the state comes out and salts it. You can't get through this pass for a month or so. It's so deep here, the sun literally never shines. It's beautiful though, isn't it? Moss is everywhere because of the dampness."

"Yes," I answered. I was concentrating on my driving. My car shifted automatically into a lower gear. I slowed our pace as we climbed. My ears stopped up.

Shapely laughed as she glanced my way. "I swear, Harley, you're nervous. You'd never make it as a hillbilly. This road is nothing. I could take you places, like over on Cliffside.

The narrow road twists around the mountain and cuts through solid rock. There's a cliff jutting out above the way and a sheer drop below.

It gets wet and slippery under the rock and if you meet another vehicle, somebody has to back up around that mountain. Believe me, that road is no place for the faint of heart.

I've heard a lot of marijuana is grown there. The lawmen just don't want to fool with the chore of finding it. Once the officers leave their cars, they have to deal with dense vines, rattlesnakes, copperheads and Lord only knows what else."

I had let Shapely talk while I concentrated on my driving skills. Finally we crested the top of the ridge. Sunlight bathed our car. I had been right, she was a country girl at heart.

My cell phone rang so I pulled off the road into the graveled lot of a little white church. I slid our windows down and turned off the engine. The air was quiet but a breeze blew through the vehicle. Shapely lifted her hair off her neck and sighed.

My phone screen showed Max was calling. "Harley, I've been trying to call you for an hour."

"I guess my signal was lost. I've been in the backwoods for awhile and in a hollow so deep."

Max cut me off. "You won't believe what has happened." He could hardly contain his excitement.

"What?"

"You know the television host, Mary McDonald? She has a show on one of the networks.

She does interviews with celebrities and newsmakers, people of interest."

"Yes," I said, growing apprehensive.

You and Shapely will be on a national show; what a break. I can't believe it; we're on the internet too. We did it, Harley, we got Woody's story to go viral. There's no stopping this thing now."

I didn't know whether to laugh or cry. "But you're the story writer, Max, won't that take away from you?"

"This is my ticket, Harley.

Mary's people said she would conclude the interview with telling her viewers to follow my story installments and she would mention me by name. What do you think?"

"I don't know. I'm a little overwhelmed."

"Ask Shapely what she thinks of it."

"All right." I turned from the phone and shared Max's information with her.

"What! Are you serious?" Shapely's face glowed.

"We will be on Mary McDonald's show? Everyone will know us, Harley. The big guys in Hollywood will see me. Where? When?" She smoothed her hair as if she was already in front of a camera then grabbed me and pressed a kiss on my cheek. "Pass that along to Max," she said. "Thank you, Max," she yelled.

I put the phone back to my ear. "Did you hear her?"

He laughed. "That was definitely an affirmative. The producers requested that Shapely dress provocatively and that you wear your collar to emphasize the contrast."

"When is this show?"

"Next week, on Wednesday. Because the subject is so timely they want to shoot as quickly as possible. You and Shapely will be paid or reimbursed for your time as they say. I will be there but not on camera."

"Where will the interview be held?"

"They're coming to you. They want to get a shot of the club and maybe a short piece of Shapely dancing, of course she'll have to keep it pretty clean, maybe when she first begins her act. I'll set it up for her apartment. We'll do a backdrop. A small crew, a couple of camera men, a makeup person and possibly a producer will be here Tuesday afternoon.

The interview will be on Wednesday afternoon at two.

Can you get your preacher clothes by Tuesday? "

"Yes, no problem."

"Great; we're all set. This is just unbelievable, Harley. This did not happen by chance. You're making a believer out of me. If ever there was divine intervention, this has to be it." Max laughed, "break after break after break. Wow."

We said our goodbyes. I turned to Shapely. She was bouncing with excitement. "I can't wait to tell my mother. I have to tell her now. We're going to be on television."

We continued on to her mother's place.

I was feeling overwhelmed. So much was happening but what good were we for Woody. So far only Shapely and Max seemed to be benefiting.

I had to admit, without them I would be nowhere in my investigation.

This had not been my plan (wait, I had no plan). At least things were happening. I had to believe they were for the best.

Shapely's mother, Daisy, was a plump happy woman in her forties who hugged her daughter and made me welcome. Her hair was a tan color and she was dressed in jeans and a top with big red roses on it. She only slightly resembled her daughter We ate the lunch of ham sandwiches and potato salad she had prepared and drank iced tea on the small back porch of her modest house.

Shapely shared her news of being on TV.

"Oh, I'm so happy for you, Dear. I know you always wanted fame. You're such a good dancer."

Shapely never once mentioned the danger she was in; nothing about the drugs or peeping tom. Her mother seemed naive and unaware; sheltered even from the unsavory side of Shapely's life. I had always heard that ignorance was bliss.

Here was proof positive. Before we left, Shapely pulled out her check book and filled in a check. I didn't see the amount.

"This should help, Mom; at least cover the house payment and insurance."

"Thanks, Honey," her mother replied. She glanced at me, almost in a contrite manner."I hate to take from Shapely but I lost my job in home health care. I was a nurse's aide. The state has cut back. I just can't seem to manage on unemployment. When that runs out, I don't know what I'll do." Her face was troubled and the check trembled in her shaking hands.

"Don't worry, Mom. Something will turn up."

Shapely gave her a hug then checked her watch. "We'd better go; gotta perform tonight."

"It was nice meeting you, Harley," Daisy said, giving me a motherly hug. "You come back for a visit any time, you hear?"

"Thank you, I hope to see you again." I made a mental note to add her to my prayer list.

We returned by a different roadway, a road much more negotiable.

"Why did you direct me in through that treacherous terrain when this way is so much nicer?"

Shapely laughed. "I just wanted you to see the real eastern Kentucky.

That's about as real as it gets. Besides it was a much closer route. I always come home that way."

"Very funny," I huffed.

The sun was setting when I pulled my vehicle into the parking lot of the Fantasy Nights Club. Shapely lifted her keys from her purse. "I'll drive home then ride back tonight with you and Max," she said as she stepped from my car.

"Okay," I replied. "I'll follow you home."

She pulled out onto the main road and I followed. The area had a speed limit and Shapely kept her pace legal. The road fell to a slight decline as we left the city limits. Shapely sped up but I wasn't concerned. I pressed my foot on the gas pedal.

Her small Chevy continued to pick up speed. *Whoa, Shapely, slow it down.*

I knew curves in the road lay ahead. She was going too fast to negotiate them safely. I tapped my horn in warning.

My heart picked up pace, racing as with the vehicle. Something was wrong. Her car picked up more speed.

Suddenly she laid her hand on her horn in a continuous blast. She was trying to tell me something. She was in trouble. Her car was out of control.

"Your brakes," I yelled although I knew she couldn't hear. *Of course she applied the brakes, they're not working.* My thoughts were growing desperate. One side of her car left the pavement. She was trying to slow it with the rough gravel on the side.

I cried, "No, Shapely, you'll lose control." She swerved then corrected. I had to do something. I remembered a cop show on TV where an officer pulled around in front of a runaway vehicle and slowed it with his. Thankfully, there was no other traffic; the time of day helped. I had to try it. The curves were advancing fast.

"God, be with us," I prayed aloud. I couldn't pause to think as I darted into the oncoming lane and sped past her. I glanced at my speed, sixty-five on this narrow country road was insane. I glanced over at Shapely. She was clutching her steering wheel, her face frozen in fear. I sped faster then swerved in front of her. I had to slow yet not cause her to collide with me. Carefully I let back on the gas. I kept glancing in my rear view mirror as her car grew closer, I saw her desperate expression. I had to pace, had to gage her speed. My body stiffened as her car grew closer and closer. She could easily lose control. I wasn't worried about myself. I had started this chain of events and couldn't let harm come to Shapely.

The curves in the road were nearing. I slowed more. Her car hit my high bumper and careened but she brought it under control "That's it, Shapely, hang on. Don't lose it." Again we collided but this time her car remained against the back end of my larger vehicle.

Gradually I slowed, hardly believing we were under control, like one unit, as if her vehicle was connected to mine. We slowed to a controllable speed then I slowed more. Finally I allowed myself to take a deep breath. My voice came out in an almost hysterical yelp of happiness. Slowly we crept off the road onto a wide bare spot of ground.

I jumped out and rushed back to Shapely and opened her door. She grabbed me as a sob burst from her."Harley, my brakes, I couldn't slow the car. Thank you, Harley, you saved my life. Oh, I could have died."

I held her and tried to quiet her."You're okay. You're safe." Slowly she calmed and wiped tears from her face. "My car is old but it's always been reliable. My brakes have been fine."

I didn't dare tell her of my suspicions. Why frighten her more unless I was sure.

"How am I going to get my car home? I can't leave it here."

"I guess we'll have to call a tow truck." A name jumped into my mind, *Howard*. He said he would help, had volunteered. I remembered he carried a .38 pistol. Right now that was a comforting thought.

He would come to our aid I was sure and he could bring my preacher clothes from the apartment closet.

I pulled my phone from my pocket and dialed his number. "Howard, I need your help."

Chapter Eighteen

We now numbered four in Shapely's small apartment. Howard had come immediately upon my request. He had located Shapely's car and towed it in.

She had calmed enough to perform her routine. Max and I had accompanied her as planned and stayed the evening. The club had operated as usual. Max and I cruised the floor, searching for anyone who acted guilty, looking for anything not in order, all the time keeping a close eye on Shapely.

We both worried about her brakes failing after the publicity. Someone had not liked what we were doing and Shapely was chosen first to pay the price.

The time was nearing 12 AM. Shapely yawned. Exhaustion was taking over me as well.

"Tomorrow I'll check out the brakes on Shapely's car," Howard said. "That's my specialty. They'll be fixed in no time."

"I don't know how to thank you, Howard," I said, "just glad you're here." I reached out and shook his hand.

"I'm happy to help out. Summer and Woody mean the world to me. I told you I'd have your backs."

Shapely smiled. "Looks like we're the four musketeers now."

Max was jotting notes on a pad.

"Howard, you take my bed tonight. I'll sleep on the sofa. You'd never fit," I said.

Howard was a tall man with a large frame.

His gaze raked the modest couch and he grinned.

"I'll take you up on that offer."

"I'll get you a pillow and quilt, Harley," Shapely said. We all said goodnight and Max closed his laptop.

Not surprisingly, we were all late sleepers the next morning. Shapely was first up. She was dressed in jeans and a tee shirt with her hair pulled back into a ponytail.

Howard had washed and groomed himself.

Max was already tapping at his laptop. I was the most disheveled. I had not slept well. I tossed and turned for the first couple of hours, my mind restless with thoughts of what could have been.

"I've got the makings of an omelet in here," Shapely said as she peered into the small refrigerator.

"Sounds great," we all agreed as we happily sipped from the hot mugs of coffee she had given us.

In her hands she gathered sausage, a pepper, onions then hash browns from the freezer.

She dropped the mass into a large skillet she pulled from a cabinet. As it sizzled and fried she beat eggs and added them. Adeptly she prepared toast to pop up just at the right time. In minutes she delivered a large portion to a plate for each of us. After a sprinkle of shredded cheese she placed our food in front of us.

"Shapely, you can cook." Max seemed shocked after his first bite. "This is delicious."

"I love to cook," she answered. "I don't just dance. I've been compiling a cookbook for years. It's Country Fare but with a twist. My recipes are tweaked with different herbs and spices, whatever I think will make the dish taste better. Most old southern dishes are good but quite bland. World spices weren't available to country folk until recent years."

"That's wonderful," I said. "You could have a second career."

"One I could be proud of?" she asked jokingly.

"Maybe, but I think I would rather cook for a husband and some kids."

"What?" Max acted stunned."I thought you wanted a dancing career and Playboy."

"I do but I know fame is fleeting and a family is forever or should be."

Howard was the first to finish his breakfast. He drained his coffee cup and rose. "I'll go check out those brakes now." He disappeared out the front door.

Shapely was next, going to her room. Max was staring at his computer screen, his face pensive. I refilled my coffee cup and sat quietly in thought.

Moments later, Howard stuck his head through the doorway. His face was pale, his eyes were large in alarm. "Hey, Harley, Max, come outside. I got to show you something." The urgency in his voice brought Max and me to our feet.

We hurried behind him toward Shapely's car.

A mat lay spread on the ground reaching beneath her vehicle. "Her brakes, her brakes." Howard took a deep breath. "They've been tampered with. A hole has been punched in the brake line."

"Are you sure?" Max's voice was incredulous.

"Yes, here, I'll show you." He dropped to the pavement. I felt a tightness in my chest. I wasn't surprised. Somehow I knew what Howard would find.

"See." Howard was pointing. Max peered under the car.

"Preacher, somebody tried to kill or do bodily harm to Shapely." Max said as he rose to his feet.

"What do we do now?" I asked Max and myself as well. I didn't know what to do or where to turn. I felt frozen with desperation. This had to stop. No more investigation, no more hunting for a killer. I had put Shapely's life in danger. Panic seized me.

What could I do? How could I stop this train I was on before it crashed.

I could not handle the danger, this new danger that had arisen. I gasped for air.

"Preacher, Preacher, get a hold of yourself.

Take deep breaths," Max coaxed as he grabbed me by the shoulders. He didn't shake me just gripped me firmly.

"Calm down. We can handle this. We'll put her in a safe place. We'll hide her. Nobody will know where she is. We'll take care of her. You and me, we can do this."

Gradually I calmed. I wasn't in this alone. I had Max and Howard. "I need to sit down."

"Let's go back inside," Howard said. He helped me onto the couch where I had tossed the night before.

Max placed another cup of coffee in my hand. "Let's all take a breather," he said. "We'll sit quietly and think." So that's what we did. We sat in silence, each of us in our own thoughts. Time passed.

I was calming which was making me tired. I laid my head back on the sofa and closed my eyes.

"What's going on?" Shapely had walked into the room.

She stood with her hands on her hips. "It's quiet as a morgue in here."

At her words we all roused and glanced at each other. Max spoke, "We have to tell her, Guys."

"Tell me what?" Shapely stiffened and lifted a hand to clutch her middle. Alarm shone in her eyes.

"I checked your brakes, Shapely. Someone damaged your brake line," Howard said.

"Are you sure?" she asked in a trembling voice.

"Yeah, I'm sure," he returned.

"Well," she said then hesitated before finishing. She straightened her shoulders and turned toward me. "Preacher, looks like it's time to talk to God. We need to thank him for watching over me and ask Him to keep us all safe. Make this a good prayer."

We all dropped to our knees and bowed our heads and poured out our hearts to the Lord.

Chapter Nineteen

Shapely's brave resolve inspired the rest of us. She went to work and did her routine. Of course we never let her out of our sight. Howard took on the role of her bodyguard, keeping his loaded handgun on him at all times.

We debated revealing the attempt on her life but Max thought it was a turning point in our investigation and needed to reveal it in his story.

Maybe he was right, because Eric, who was high on our list of suspects, made a strange move. He strode over and stood uncomfortably before us one night. He flexed his shoulder muscles and stepped nervously from foot to foot. He clenched his hands together in front forming a v with his arms. His stance reminded me of a soldier. With his build, maybe he was a former marine.

"Guys, can I talk to you for a minute?" he asked.

I know Max was as shocked as I but he calmly said, "Sure, Eric, have a chair and join us." The bouncer pulled out a chair which seemed too small for him, then sat down on it.

He cleared his throat. "I read your piece about Shapely's car brakes being damaged. I want to help protect her. I think she needs a bodyguard."

"She has bodyguards, in fact, she has three," Max answered.

"But I'm strong. I could cold cock anybody who tried to touch her. I failed Carrie. I tried in my way. I kept watch here at the club." His eyes were troubled and he pleaded. "There are monsters in this place, capable of animal acts. I've been around them long enough to know."

"What do you mean, you kept an eye on Shapely and Carrie?" I asked.

"Well." He glanced around then leaned in over the table closer to us. "I have a way of checking their rooms. Their doors have slip bolt locks from the inside once they enter their rooms, but the actual keys could get into some awful hands and I mean awful." His expression was one of disgust. "I always tried to check their rooms before they entered to make sure no one lay in wait for them. Nobody bothered them here. I would have broken their backs if they had tried." Eric gave his big hands a twisting motion. "I couldn't help Carrie after she left the club but I have a chance with Shapely. I can watch her all the time if you two will let me." His eyes pleaded with honest appeal .I care about her more than you know.

Max and I stared at one another, for a moment, speechless. Eric was a gentle giant.

It took awhile for the realization that Eric's use of the loft (unorthodox as it was) was a protective gesture, if we could believe him and I did. He took his job seriously, maybe too seriously, he was a bouncer, a protector.

Max's voice was firm. "Look, Eric, we do appreciate your concern for Shapely, and if we felt we needed you, we certainly would say so. You would definitely be an asset."

Eric smiled. Max had let him down easy.

"These awful hands you refer to, is that someone in particular?

Is there someone we should make note of as our suspects?" I asked. Eric knew the patrons of the club better than Max or I ever could. Shapely said he had worked there for over five years.

"Manos and his henchmen, there's nothing they won't do. They've got no souls, none of them. I swear they are the spawn of the devil himself. I heard one of them betrayed Manos." Eric hesitated and checked to see who might be within earshot. He lowered his tone. "They skinned him alive then threw him in the river.

Yeah, his poor bones are probably laying on the bottom of the mighty Ohio right now. I work for the man and do as I'm told. I'm not taking any chances. You don't cross the likes of these men, believe me."

"Thanks, Eric." Max said and I affirmed.

"If we need help we'll let you know."

Eric nodded his head and rose from our table.

"Do you have your list?" Max asked me.

"Yes," I said and pulled out the folded piece of paper. "I know what to do." I retrieved my pen and marked through Eric's name. "Our list is getting short."

"Who's left?" Max asked. I glanced over the few names remaining.

"There's Alfred Dugall, Carrie's stepfather.

Mr. Wallace, the club manager remains and the two names that Manos added. We're quickly running out of suspects".

You know, there's a chance the killer isn't even on this list. We may have skipped someone "Wait a minute, didn't Howard say Alfred Dugall is in jail for beating up Carrie's mother?"

"Yes he did, so he couldn't have tampered with Shapely's brakes." I unfolded my paper again and drew a line through his name. "We're down to three names, Max." I thought of what Eric had told us, about a man being skinned alive and thrown into the river. We were dealing with the worst of the worst. A chill rolled over my body and I shook. Were Max and I prepared to deal with the results of our prying? Were we kidding ourselves?

Thoughts of the rolling murky depths of the Ohio River took hold and I couldn't get it out of my head.

"What's wrong, Harley?" Max asked. "You look a little pale." Concern creased his face.

"Do you think we might be in over our heads, Max?"

"Of course we are," he replied, "murderers, dope dealers." He chuckled. "Sure is exciting, isn't it?" Max tried to make it light then his face sobered. "We're going to do this, Harley. Don't let doubt creep in. These are just people like us only a little meaner. Everybody makes mistakes. There's no such thing as a perfect crime. We're going to find that mistake. Remember we have Howard and his .38."

"Yes, thank God for Howard." I was not a man of violence but I believed in protecting one's self. How could the thought of a weapon bring a feeling of peace. I was learning things about myself.

Chapter Twenty

Wednesday arrived. The time was nearing for the interview. A team from the Mary McDonald's show had arrived. They filmed Shapely performing her dance routine at the club. We had cleared it with Manos. During the filming, he nor any of his men were about.

The crew gave us instructions and let us know what to expect. Shapely spent the morning in the bathroom (her dressing room). Occasionally she would appear with rollers in her hair and grab a Coke or a sandwich and then hurry back to dressing. She didn't seem nervous, just excited. I, on the other hand was growing more anxious with each minute. What was Mary going to ask us? I felt unprepared. A sudden thought hit me. I hadn't told Beth. Sweat popped out on my brow.

How long had it been since I had talked to her? I couldn't remember. I had been so involved I had forgotten my wife.

I pulled at my white-collar. I hadn't worn it in so long, it felt unnatural. What was happening to me? Just a case of nerves, I tried to reassure myself.

Finally, the crew arrived.

Howard had left early to go home and attend to his business. The crew consisted of two producers and a cameraman. They went about making a set for us by pulling the small kitchen table over in front of a solid wall.

"Shapely, it's time," Max called. He made a point of remaining in the background. When Shapely walked out, she was wearing a gold low-cut dress which brought out the golden highlights in her hair. The cameraman gave a low whistle in appreciation. "Thank you," she said, then blew him a kiss. She was going to be the star of this show for sure.

A producer rigged us with small microphones with wires they ran too small packs she had attached at our backs. The other producer, named Greta, unsnapped a small case. She retrieved a powder puff. "My, preacher, you're perspiring." She patted my face with powder. "There, now you're ready," she said. "Somebody turn down the temperature; we don't want him sweating during the shoot. The two of you will sit at the table," Greta said with authority in her voice.

Great, I thought, *I'll have some place to put my hands*. I was ill at ease and it showed.

"No, no, the table will hide my dress, my body, my legs. The table will hide me, Shapely Shaw," she pouted.

What a time to turn into a diva, I thought.

Max walked over rubbing his chin in a thoughtful pose.

"You know, she's right. This is about the preacher and the stripper.

Your audience will want to see them, really see them." He picked up the table and carried it across the room, then returned and positioned our chairs.

"Shapely, you sit here," he said.

Shapely obeyed. Max angled her a little to the side. "Now cross your legs," he said. She did. He helped to put her in a more flattering pose. He fluffed her hair with his hands.

"Remember, I'm a photographer, I have a trained eye."

He turned to me, "Preacher, you can face the camera. I want you to look directly at the audience." He grabbed my shoulders and shook me slightly. "Relax, you're going to do great." Max smiled and I felt better. The producer stood perplexed, allowing Max free reign." How's that?" He turned and asked them.

"Uh, looks great," they agreed.

"Okay, now all we have to do is wait for the cue from the show." Max again receded into the background.

The audio was turned on in our ears. It seemed strange to conduct an interview remotely. I would have been more comfortable talking to the interviewer personally. I cleared my throat. Mary McDonnell was giving her audience background info about our story. She first told of Woody and his circumstance then she talked about Carrie and her murderer then she turned her attention to us.

"There has been a remarkable turn in the story because of two people I'm about to introduce.
 I'm sure most of you have followed their story which has been covered by Max Holmes, a photojournalist. He is recording their journey for a readership of millions.

They are Shapely Shaw and Rev. Harley Daniels, you may know them as the preacher and the stripper. Together they've taken up Woody's cause and are determined to prove his innocence.

May I introduce Rev. Harley Daniels and Ms. Shapely Shaw. Thank you for being with us." We waited until the resounding applause ended.

The producer gave us our cue. "Thank you for having us," I said.

"Yes, we're glad to be with you," Shapely added.

"How did you learn of Woodrow Pierce, a prisoner on death row in Eddyville prison?"

I explained the circumstance of my church work, my visit with Woody and my certainty of his innocence. "What is the name of your church?"

"The Trinity Way Church." Immediately I thought of the congregation and the disapproving board of directors. I hoped they didn't mind me mentioning the church by name. I was caught and had to respond truthfully.

"Your congregation must be very understanding for you to spend so much time on the case."

"Yes, I have a congregation of wonderful people.
 They gave me a two month sabbatical to work on the case." My cheeks grew warm.

"They must be very proud of their pastor," Mary said

"I hope so," I replied.

"Shapely," Mary turned her attention to my partner. "How did you get involved?"

Shapely drew a deep breath. " I dance at the same club where Carrie worked. She and I were friends.

I testified at Woody's trial and I don't think I was questioned properly. I feel my words were taken out of context and may have harmed Woody's defense, so I think I owe him."

"We are certain Woody is innocent. I think we might be getting close to the real killer," I said.

The interviewer replied, "I was informed that the brakes on Shapely's car had been sabotaged."

Shapely answered, " Yes. Evidently that took place on the night before I drove to visit my mother, which I do on the same day each week. The route I take is treacherous. I would have lost control and undoubtedly have crashed, but on this day Rev. Daniels drove me. I think God was watching over us."

Mary McDonnell gasped. "I think the two of you are wonderfully brave and I wish you success. I would like to help so I have a surprise for you."

Shapely and I exchanged puzzled glances. "Famed attorney, Roberto Martin has volunteered his services. He will look at Woody's case and handle his appeal." At that point Mr. Martin joined Mary on stage. We heard their conversation.

He said he was happy to review Woody's trial transcript and appeal his sentence.

They turned their attention back to us. We thanked Mrs. McDonnell and the famous lawyer for their support and aid. Our conversation continued for a few more minutes then we were dismissed.

"That's a wrap," Greta said. She and the others began removing our mikes.

"How did we do?" Shapely asked.

"You were wonderful." The cameraman answered. We thanked each other then within minutes they had gathered their equipment and were headed for the nearest airport.

"Now what?" Shapely asked, as she ran her hand down her golden dress. "Do I just wait around for the killer to strike again? Next time he might succeed."

After the excitement of the interview she seemed to have fallen into a mood near depression.

Max grabbed the table and then the chairs putting them back to their original position. " Sit down you two, there has to be a next logical step. Let's talk about it." We sat in silence. Finally, Max said, "Harley, let's see your list again."

By now the piece of paper was showing signs of wear. I gently unfolded it and handed it to Max.

"We still have three names," Max said. First, the club manager, Mr. Wallace."

"Wait," Shapely stopped him. "Why do you have him on your list?"

"He was a logical choice, we thought," I said.

"He wouldn't hurt a flea," Shapely said with a dismissive wave of her hand.

"Are you sure?" I asked. "We know he's dipping into the till. Maybe Carrie found out and he got scared she would tell Manos."

Shapely shook her head in a negative way. " No, I've known him too long. He gambles, always thinking he's going to strike it rich at the casino up the road a ways.

He does a lot that I don't like, but kill Carrie - no way. You can cross him off."

"All right," I said. "We trust your opinion."

"There are only two people left," Max said. Carlos Garcia and Alfonzo Cortez." He tapped his pen on the table. " A next step, there is a next step." Silence settled around us. We were all deep in thought. Finally, Max looked at me.

"What was it Carrie said to you in that dream you had?"

I thought back in an attempt to recapture her words. Again I saw her floating above me, hair billowing around her beautiful face. "Check my thesis. She said check my thesis."

Max pondered the words and looked toward me.

"Do we know if she presented the thesis?"

"No," I said simply.

"She hadn't," Shapely added. " She was writing it when she was killed. I know because she was struggling with it."

"What was the subject of the work?" Max asked.

"I know the title," she said.

Max and I stared at her, waiting for her to finish. "Well? The title?"

"Criminal Behavior," Shapely said. "She was studying someone, a person she knew was the subject of her paper. She was debating environmental influences versus natural instinct.

Also the possibility of inherited traits. It was a bit complicated to me. I just think people are what they want to be. Each is responsible for his actions, period. She wanted to make everyone complex."

I appreciated Shapely's simplistic approach but knew through studies that the human psyche was more complicated than that.

Max sat stunned then he slapped his hand down on the table. His face glowed with excitement. "We've got it. We've got the killer. He's the one she was going to expose. Criminal is the keyword. If she exposed criminal acts, that could mean prison or death if the crimes were bad enough. Why didn't we see that?" He slapped his forehead in exasperation. "We had the clue all the time." I was just as stunned as Max.

"But the police searched her laptop," Shapely reminded us. "They evidently found nothing suspicious."

"Well, maybe the killer deleted the work." I wasn't the most knowledgeable in electronics but the delete key was evident.

Max spoke in a deflated voice. "I'm sure the police have a recovery program. They should have viewed everything she ever put in the machine."

"Maybe if they didn't recognize they had evidence. Perhaps they glanced over the document as a class project, not realizing what they had," I said.

"That seems possible to me," Max replied.

"Personally, I think that could easily happen; after reading the trial transcript, which was a joke. How could the jury ever convict someone with no evidence? If he were guilty he would not have been so stupid as to leave his DNA all over. A smart killer would have made sure there was nothing to connect him, no mask, no clothes. They should have realized that. Sorry," I apologized. "I just get so heated when I think about that transcript. I hope that lawyer, Martin, tears that trial apart."

"In the meantime we have things to do. Shapely, can you direct us to Carrie's mother's place?"

"Yes," she said, seeming renewed. "I'll call her and say we're coming. I'll just go change my clothes."

"I'll call Howard," Max said," and tell him we'll meet him at the apartment tonight."

I pulled off my collar. I would change to jeans. They were much more comfortable. More or less, we rode in silence stopping only for a Coke and burger.

We seemed to be on a mission, like we were nearing the end of a long journey.

Soon we were driving up the graveled rutted lane to the house where Carrie had grown up. The place was in disrepair with peeling yellow paint and green shutters hanging askew. A broken window was held together by a piece of masking tape. The lawn lay untended and was littered with overgrown weeds.

It was evident that a child growing up under such dire circumstance would not have been able to afford a college education. Carrie had needed money.

The way she chose to make it though, took her young life.

We three stood on the porch, careful not to step through it where boards had broken and given way.

Shapely rapped on the door and called out," Marybelle, this is Shapely and two friends, we would like to talk to you, please."

A gaunt figure in a simple patterned housedress cautiously pulled the door open. The woman had fair skin and gray hair pulled back with a rubber band. Streaks of honey color wove through her long locks. At an earlier time she would have been a beauty just like her daughter."Come in and make yourselves at home," she said.

A recent cut that had been stitched up marred her cheekbone. She shuffled her feet gingerly like her body was sore.

My heart went out to her. I wanted to comfort her.

Shapely introduced us and we shook hands. Hers was bony and cold to the touch. "I'm sorry about the loss of your daughter, Mrs.Simpson," was all I could think to say.

"Have a seat," she said. Max and I each found a worn chair on which to sit. Shapely joined the lady on a broken down green sofa. I glanced around the room. It seemed almost a shrine to Carrie. Assorted photos at different ages adorned the walls and school photos in colored frames sat on the tables.

"My Little Carrie Ann, I'll never get over losing her. There just ain't no justice in this world.

First my girl gets murdered then they put Woody in prison. He was like a son to me. I wanted to testify for him but his lawyer wouldn't let me, said I wasn't needed, that I couldn't help him." She wiped away a tear.

Max was quietly taking notes. "Mrs. Simpson, would it be okay for us to look at Carrie's computer?"

"Yes," she answered, "anything to help catch the real killer." She said in explanation, "I've been following your story just like everybody else. I never seen the like of people who call me about it."

She led us into an adjoining room."Here," she said, pointing to a laptop."I've been keeping it charged up just in case you might need it.

I hoped you might come visiting so I could thank you."

"That's very thoughtful of you," Max said. He unplugged the unit and carried it back into the living room and placed it on the coffee table. Quickly he stroked key after key. "Nothing has been installed to search for hidden files." He kept tapping keys. "There's a lot of material in here but nothing about her thesis. "Hey", he cried, "a locked program. Mrs. Simpson, do you know the password for this?"

"Heavens no," she said. " I don't even know how to turn the thing on. That technical stuff is for you young folk."

"Password, password." Max was mumbling to himself as he tried different combinations he thought might work. "This is hopeless," he finally said as he fell back on the sofa.

"We're missing something, I can feel it. Think Harley, what are we missing?"

Mentally I went over all that had happened since meeting Carrie in spirit form, the club, the cast of characters, especially Juan Manos. Something caught - Carrie's room at the club. Manos took us into her room. We searched everywhere. A feeling of pure elation rushed through me. My face flushed. I jumped to my feet.

I had two pairs of jeans so I had a 50-50 chance that what I wanted was in my pocket. My fingers closed around a small folded piece of paper. I pulled it out. "Remember this?" I asked, my voice shaking.

"We found it in a pocket of a leather jacket of Carrie's ... in her room, at the club."

"Yes, of course." Max's excitement matched my own. He took it from my hand and read the letters aloud, "secficb. What could the letters stand for? We all reviewed the letters.

"Maybe secret file?" I questioned. "Sec fi. But cb? Criminal behavior? We're just guessing. If only the letters were the killer's name."

"This has to be it." Quickly Max tapped the password on the keys and the program opened. "We've got it, we've got it." Max jumped up and shouted. He grabbed Shapely then me. The three of us hopped like excited kids.

"I'll get this on a memory stick then we can study it at leisure. He did the task then shut down the computer and handed it to Carrie's mom. "If this writing of Carrie's tells us what I think it will, we may have a chance at cracking this case. We will keep our fingers crossed."

"Oh, praise God." The mother cried. "I been praying for something like this. I want true justice for my little girl. Thank you, thank you so much."

We said goodbye and each received a hug from Mrs. Simpson. Our mood was much better on our return trip. Max turned on the radio to a local station featuring the strings of bluegrass. Shapely sang along, knowing all the words. Max appeared as awestruck as I.

"Shapely," I declared. "You missed your calling. You have a fabulous voice. First, the cooking and now the singing, you're multitalented.

"Yes, but I'm just a little uneducated country girl. Nobody is going to pay attention to me. But they pay attention to Shapely Shaw."

"By the way, what was your real given name?" Max asked.

"Do you really want to know?"

"Of course," he answered.

"Well, my mother is a fan of country music. She had a favorite song called Little Liza Jane. So I used to be Liza Jane Shaw." She giggled. "Can you believe it? Liza Jane?"

"I've never heard of the song," Max stated. "How does it go?"

Shapely began to sing, "Little Liza, Little Liza Jane, hey, Little Liza, Little Liza Jane, what's your name, pretty little thing, where do you live, nigh down the lane, Oh, Little Liza, Little Liza Jane."

Soon Max and I learned the words and joined her in song. We were happy. We had our answer, our prize. All was well as we headed back to the Badlands and a killer. Little did we know what awaited. For these minutes all was lost in the joy of singing.

Chapter Twenty-one

Howard called and said he was running a little late but would try to meet us at the club. A sense of fear tightened my insides. Without Howard we had no real protection. We all were anxious to see what Carrie had written. Everything was riding on her words.

First Max uploaded it then connected to Shapely's printer. He printed three copies, one for each of us so we wouldn't be crowding each other around his laptop.

Carrie hadn't gotten past an outline and jotted thoughts, not yet a completed work. We each read silently then we all wanted to share what we had found.

"She doesn't say who she's writing about, isn't that what we need?" Shapely complained.

"No, it would have been too easy if she had named names," I said, disappointment evident in my tone.

"Let's break it apart and analyze," Max stated. He read-

Criminal Behavior - I submit that the result has environmental causes and inherited traits-the subject was once an innocent cooing baby held in his mother's arms. Observation-at this stage of life no evidence of criminal behavior is present. He enters school, an overweight child from a poor home, he has no shoes to wear like other children. He is teased and bullied, he learns to survive, he must fight. My observation-at this point- he has, instead of building character, in my opinion, built resentment. A turning point? He witnesses his mother being beaten then shot and killed by his father-my observation he chooses to unleash anger upon society, the cause is environmental and an inherited trait, as a teenager he forms a gang-is the ruthless

leader. He learns to wield power and others will do his bidding, he
lives by gang mentality into adulthood. notes- read the Journal of
Modern Psychology on subject call and interview, Dr. Samuel LeBrun
on subject.

        We all sat in silence, shoulders slumped, deflated, like balloons
after the party." She didn't tell us," I said, "she didn't let us know who
her subject was. She could have been writing about anyone. What do
we do now? I feel like we hit a brick wall."

        "We've one option. In my next installment, I can mention
Carrie's thesis. I'll say we can't discern who she's talking about but
think there must be hidden clues that we will discover later. Readers
like suspense. Maybe that will force the killer to act."

        Shapely and I exchanged anxious glances. "Do we want the
killer to act? What will he do? We don't want to force him to kill
again. Max, we've got to use caution here."

        "We need him to get spooked and do something to reveal
himself." Max seemed so nonchalant. Did he have no sense of fear?
This was not fiction he was writing. We were playing with our lives. I
had enough fear for both of us. Where was Howard? He should have
been here by now. As if on cue, Howard walked through the door.

        "Boy, am I glad to see you." Shapely cried. " I didn't want to go
to work without you. I'm frightened, Howard. Do you have your
gun?"

        "Well, it sure feels nice to be needed," he laughed. He lifted his
vest to reveal the gun in a holster.

        We caught him up on the day's events then we had a light
supper and headed for the Fantasy Nights club. The evening was a
night of sameness. I was growing weary of the club scene, too much
noise, too much liquor, too much smoke and most of all too much skin.

        Oh, I had such a longing to see Beth. For a moment I allowed
my mind to go back, before I got involved in Woody's case. My life
had been so simple, so comfortable. I stepped outside the club where it
was quiet then I pulled out my cell phone. I rang her number. My heart
picked up pace. "Hello Harley," she said. " How are you?"

She sounded so good, so precious to me. I found it difficult to speak, but when I did the words gushed from me. " I love you so much".

"Oh Harley, I love you too. Come home. Stop this crusade you're on. I'm worried. I'm so afraid for you. I've been following the story by Max. You are in danger. You're all in danger."

"I know. I really feel it now. I've not only endangered myself but others as well. If I leave, Beth, they will still be in danger. We've revealed too much. The killer has already acted once by sabotaging Shapely's car.

He wasn't successful that time. Next time he may be. I'm just trusting in God's will."

"I've really been calling on my faith too. I pray for you every night."

"By the way, Shapely and I will be featured on Mary McDonald's show tomorrow."

"Mary McDonald? Really? That's big, Harley.

You really are trying hard to free Woody, aren't you."

"Yes Beth."

"Well, I really admire you for that, Harley. I know I wasn't very cooperative but I'm proud of you. I'll watch you tomorrow and I'll call Janice too. I want her to see what she and the church dismissed, the most honorable man they could ever hope to have serve them. Just wait, we'll show them. You'll catch that killer. You will be in demand. Everyone will be wanting the famous Reverend Harley Daniels as their pastor."

"Thank you, Beth. This will be over soon and I'll come home to you and no more crusades. I promise." We said our goodbyes. I felt my heart grow lighter. My wife had come through for me. She was on my side and so was God. I felt renewed and strong.

I needed to speak with my Lord. I walked through the parking lot to a grassy knoll.The area was illuminated by the garish gold colored lighted stars of the club behind me.

I fell to my knees and dropped my head and closed my eyes in prayer. I thanked my Lord for allowing me to serve him and do his will. I promised him to do my best.

Chapter Twenty-two

Max was busy on his laptop. When I walked into the room he hesitated and looked at me with emotion in his cool gray eyes that I didn't understand.

"What's up?" I asked.

"I've been a photographer for many years and never have I captured an image like last night. I followed you, Harley. I was concerned, thought you needed a shoulder. I... I saw you praying and my natural instinct was to take a photo. Look at what I captured."

He twisted the laptop around toward me. I caught my breath. My figure was kneeling in prayer and around me were rays of golden light streaming from the stars around the block building behind me. A glow encased my figure. "That is an extraordinary picture," I said. I felt in awe. He had captured the essence of my faith and my battle.

"For a photographer this is a once in a lifetime occurrence.I couldn't have set this picture up. This is award-winning, Harley. This installment will be a feature."

"I'm happy for you Max. You should be rewarded for all you are doing."

"Thanks, preacher. I'll get this off to the publisher," he said.

The story of our finding Carrie's writings was published. The next day about noon we heard a knock at the door. I opened it. Pure fear squeezed my heart for an instant for there stood three of Manos's men. "Come in," I said, not knowing what else to say. They walked inside and closed the door behind them. Max and Howard were in the room with me. Hearing the voices, Shapely came out of her room.

"Manos wants us to escort you four to the club, pronto," one said in a thick accent.

"Why?" Shapely asked bravely." I have to get ready for my show tonight."

"Show no matter. Manos wants you all now and bring with you the paper Carrie wrote."

"Do we have a choice?" Max asked.

"No." Was the man's blunt answer. They put two of us as passengers in Shapely's car and two in the vehicle they drove. I shared the back seat with Shapely. She reached out and clutched my hand, her eyes were widened with fear. I tried to reassure her with a smile.

The club was empty when we arrived. I looked around for Eric, even his presence would have been reassuring. We were herded back through the hallway to the small office.

Before we entered we were searched. Howard groaned when they found and removed his gun. We crowded into the room with the door closing solidly after us. Behind the desk sat Manos. His arms were folded on the desk. His face was reddened with silent rage, his body rocked nervously.

"Hey, writer," he demanded. "I want the paper my Carrie was writing. Read it to me."

"Okay, Sir." Max handed him a copy.

I searched the room with my gaze. Max was nervous but he was not the only one. One of Manos's men was sweating bullets and he was breathing hard.

Max began reading, first the title then her first observation. Shapely scooted closer to me. I put my arm around her. I would protect her with my life. Poor girl, this was more than she had bargained for.

Again I thought of the dark rolling waters of the Ohio River. Darn Eric, I wished he had never mentioned such a fate.

When Max read the part about school then leading a gang, Manos suddenly slammed a fist down on the desk top. "My Carrie, my little Carrie was writing about me. Why, why." He exclaimed an expletive. This brute of a man seemed almost near tears. "Read on, please," he said. Max continued and read about the young man who witnessed his mother being killed by his father. Manos sat stunned for a moment. I could see he was searching his mind. He held up his hand. "Wait," he cried. "Read... read that part again." Max complied. "No one knew about that, no one. I told nobody except.." His gaze roamed the room and settled on his man Carlos, the one who was perspiring heavily. "I told you, Carlos, only you. You mad dog, you were the one giving Carrie my story.

You murderer of women." Manos rose from his chair and pointed a finger at the man. "You had my back, you said." He advanced toward him like an animal ready to devour its prey. We stood in stunned silence. We were watching a bad movie, surely we could not witness what we knew we were seeing.

"You are the monster who killed my Carrie, my beautiful innocent girl. She would never hurt you or anyone. Why? Why?" His last plea was almost a sob as his voice broke.

Desperation flashed from Carlos's eyes. He knew he was caught and made a desperate move. He grabbed Shapely and dragged her close against his body, then from nowhere he pulled a switchblade knife. Shapely screamed as he brought the knife to her throat. Her eyes gave a desperate plea to Max, Howard and me but we were helpless.

"Why?" Manos demanded again.

"She wouldn't let me have her." Carlos broke, spewing a defiant confession to Manos's demanding presence. "I helped her. She needed to know about you Manos. She wanted to know why you were so bad. She wanted to fix you. She wanted to take the evil out of your heart so she could care for you. She couldn't love you, Manos. I should have been paid for my help. All I wanted was for her to give herself to me freely. But she refused, she laughed at me. So I showed her, nobody laughs at Carlos Garcia". He stared into Manos's enraged face who appeared as a raging bull, ready to charge. Carlos pushed the knife against Shapely's throat. "I kill this one too if you come near."

Tension in the air was palatable.

"You'll never get away, Carlos. I will hunt you till the end of the earth and you will suffer as you have never suffered," Manos said.

While the confrontation was at its peak, from the corner of my eye, I saw a movement directly above Carlos's head.

A panel was slowly and quietly being lifted. Carlos was so enraged he didn't notice. Shapely was whimpering like a child, careful not to move lest the knife pierce her.

I furtively stole another glance. Eric squatted on the beams near the opening in the ceiling. *Act Eric*, I thought. *The time is now. Don't hesitate.* Max, Howard and I were useless to the situation. We were helpless bystanders. I knew Eric needed to make a drop now before Carlos changed his position and he did.

His aim was exact. He jumped; one foot striking the arm that held the knife to Shapely's throat. He hit the arm hard with one foot, knocking the knife from Carlos's hand. It slid across the floor. All three figures went down. Shapely screamed, the two men grunted. They wrestled but Eric was more muscular and easily restrained the smaller figure. Manos and Alfonzo grabbed Carlos before he could rise. Shapely scrambled out of their way. Max and I grabbed her and pulled her close to us. She sobbed in relief.

Carlos struggled for his life but he was overpowered. Alfonzo threw a grinding punch to Carlos's jaw. A cracking noise resounded through the room and he slumped, stunned. Manos was quick to grab him. He added his own punishment by slapping the offender repeatedly, first one cheek then the other until Carlos was reeling then he threw a powerful fist to Carlos's middle. A cry burst from him and he slumped.

Manos turned and kicked the switchblade toward us. "I'm sure you will find Carrie's blood residue on the blade and this dog's fingerprints on the handle.

You will say you found it hidden outside the motel where Carrie died. Your friend, Woody will be freed. The police will search for this guilty asshole but he will not be found."

185

I had to object. "Manos, please consider the legitimate justice system for Carlos."

"Listen, Mr. preacher man, I told you we have our own justice system. I will see that your Woody is free." He pointed a finger at me then he moved it to encompass us all. "Remember, we don't exist. Is that clear?"

Max placed his arm across my chest, thinking he had to restrain me. "We all understand, don't we?" He turned and looked at our small hovering group. Shapely, Howard, Max and I nodded our heads. Yes, we all agreed. "We understand."

"Preacher, you can say a prayer for Carlos, but silently. I do not want to hear." What else could I do? I had to play by Manos's rules. I had no choice. So I lowered my head and appealed for fairness in Carlos's judgment.

Manos slapped Eric on the back. "Good work. You have gained my gratitude. I will take care of you."

"Thank you, Eric," Shapely added, her voice breaking. He just smiled at her in return.

"You can all be excused and gracias." Manos said. He added, "Don't forget the evidence you found." I picked up a manila envelope lying on the desk then stooped and pushed the knife inside it.

Manos stood in front of Carlos."Remember, Carlos, the hombre who dared to cross Manos?"

"Si," the terrified man responded. Manos grabbed the front of his shirt and pushed his face close.

"You taught us the art of disposal very well. I will enjoy yours, as much as you enjoyed his." Manos pressed his finger to Carlos's forehead. "You started here and advanced this way." He ran his finger over the helpless man's head and down the back of his neck.

"You peeled him like an onion, a bloody, screaming onion, am I right, amigo?"

Shapely moaned and slumped in my arms. She had fainted.

"No, Manos, no, I beg you, I will do anything, anything, no dispose me, please." Carlos cried out in fear as he pleaded for his life. I could not witness and had to turn away. Shapely made Manos realize he still had an audience.

He turned and screamed at us, his face still reddened with rage. "I said you were excused and remember we don't exist. Now go freely before I change my mind."

Eric herded us out of the office."Count yourselves lucky," he said to us, "not everyone is allowed to leave. Please forget everything you saw and heard. Your lives depend on it. Manos means what he says.

Don't ever cross him." Eric escorted us from the club then handed Howard's gun back to him. Howard took Shapely from my arms which was a relief for I was struggling. He had much more physical strength than I. We were free to leave and walked silently to Shapely's car.

Chapter Twenty-three

We all slept late the next morning. The afternoon before seemed unreal. We finally gathered together after coffee to discuss what to do next. Max turned on his laptop. In a moment he yelled in excitement. "I told you, I told you. Your photo went crazy, Harley. Listen to this-headline, The Photo Seen Around The World. Captured, a Moment of Good Versus Evil". We took a moment to relish the notoriety, then we sobered.

"What are we going to do about the knife?" Shapely asked, bringing us back to earth. She was still shaken and pale from the night before. In fact, I think we all were.

For a moment Max's face looked puzzled."We have to go to the motel and do a search. We have to find a likely place where Carlos could have hidden the knife. A site where the police might not have checked, and where it would have been protected from the elements."

"We actually revealed the murderer and can't say a word about it," Howard said.

"But we have something better to free Woody; we have the weapon. It could not get better than that," Max answered. " Let's eat breakfast out then hit the motel. I've got a great story installment to write, then I'll contact the lawyer. What's his name?" Max looked at me.

"Martin," I said. "With this evidence and that damaging trial transcript this deal is done. No, let's not get too sure of ourselves. Everybody knock on wood," I said, recalling the many times sure things were not so sure.

The motel was just as I remembered, white cinder block with faded blue shutters. "Gee," Shapely said. "I can't see Carrie staying here, but she did watch her expenses, I guess her education meant everything to her."

"I didn't know the girl but I feel that I did and I admire her determination," Howard said.

We exited the car. Max said, " Now where would our murderer hide his weapon? It has to be a place where the police wouldn't have looked."

We all did a visual search of the building. We walked closer for a better inspection. Only one car was in the lot.

I assumed it belonged to the manager. There were no patrons to disturb.

Behind the building was a small room added on. It had been built for years. The roof slanted downward and was not enclosed with a soffit.

"Perfect," Max said. We all laughed as he walked over and placed the plastic enclosed knife up on the open wall ledge. We each stepped back and checked, it was well hidden.

"Well," Max said as he walked over and retrieved a switchblade, " look what I found, evidence for sure."

"Perfect," we agreed.

"What are you people doing back here?" The manager stormed around the corner of the building. The scrawny old man carried a broken baseball bat. "Oh, it's you," he said, losing his threatening tone when he recognized me.

"We were just looking around," I said.

"What's that you're holding there?" He asked Max.

"We found this knife hidden up on the eve," Max said, pointing to the open space beneath the roof.

"Well, I'll be danged," Mr. Adkins said. "You reckon that knife killed that young woman last year and it's been laying up there all that time?"

"I reckon so," Max answered in an amused tone. "We just found it."

I was thankful Max was telling the needed lie and not me.

"You know, I don't remember the police looking back here after the murder. They went over the room real good, and they searched the lot and them shrubs a'growin' out there in front but they never come back here. I guess it's a good thing you did."

"Yes it is," I answered.

The manager turned and headed back toward his office, his curiosity satisfied.

"I guess my next installment is written. We should be ready to head back to the apartment."

"That was easy," Shapely said.

"We've got to contact Woody's attorney and get this evidence to him for testing," Max said.

When we got back to Shapely's, her cell phone rang so she went to her room to answer then Howard's rang and he excused himself. Max was busy typing, that left me alone to think.

Now, everything depended on a residue of Carrie's blood remaining on the knife and the attorney being as good as his reputation. Woody had to benefit, either by a new trial or a stay of execution. A release was almost too much to hope for. With all the publicity, the governor had to be aware of the case. How fortunate I was to run into Max when I did. Without him I felt I could not have achieved my goal. Then it hit me, there had to be a higher power behind our meeting. I felt an immediate leap of faith.

I was not in control.

This had to work because it was meant to happen My cell phone rang. It was Beth.

Her voice sang with excitement, "Oh, Harley, you won't believe what has happened. Janice called me. The church committee held a meeting. The congregation demanded that they want you back. She said they apologized and would be proud to have you as their pastor."

I was surprised, even shocked and slow to respond. "That is quite a change of mind. Are you sure?"

"Yes, Janice promised. She is so sorry, Harley. She said they really didn't give you a chance. They didn't know how deep your convictions were. They are so proud that you did what you did in spite of them.

She talked like you would get a raise too. Isn't that wonderful? She'll send you a formal letter."

"Yes, it is wonderful. It is just what I always wanted, a congregation that understands me and appreciates my convictions. I would never purposely let them down."

"I know, Harley, that's why I love you."

A lump rose in my throat. My life was falling back into place. But what about Woody's case? We had to know about the blood-stained knife. I said goodbye to Beth with the feeling that we would be together soon.

Max had stepped out and when he returned he said, "I next-day aired the weapon to Mr. Martin. We talked earlier. The attorney said that if Carrie's DNA and someone else's, other than Woody, was on the knife, this case is settled. He is going to pull strings and get this test done as quickly as possible. We just have to wait and I have to write. I want to thank you, Harley, for telling me Woody's story. You have made my career. I'm getting offers from all the TV networks. One company wants to give me my own investigative show, a lesser-known production company, but hey, my own show."

I laughed with joy for my new friend who had worked so diligently by my side. "You deserve whatever you want, Max. One day I will be able to say, 'I know that man.'

"That famous writer/reporter?" I'll be asked from a disbelieving person, and I'll say, yes, and show them your story about Shapely and me."

"Don't." Max held up his hand. " I can't let this all go to my head."

The TV had been on but was on low volume. At least two hundred people were gathered with signs. They chanted, "Free Woody, free Woody now." They switched their words to, "free the innocent man, free the innocent man," then "catch the real killer, catch the real killer."

I was the first to notice," Max, it seems a lot of demonstrators in that group appear to be Hispanic. Do you agree?"

"Yes, I guess that's politics. There's a podium. I think our lawyer friend is going to speak; More publicity, that Manos is a genius."

Two women and one man stood at the podium. A lady stepped forward and raised her hand to silence the crowd, then she introduced Mr. Martin. The well-dressed man was an imposing figure, tall and impeccably groomed and in an obviously expensive gray pin-striped suit and pale gray shirt with a red tie.

"I called a news conference today to inform you wonderful people of Eastern Kentucky that I am working to free your innocent son, Woodrow Howard Pierce. After reviewing his trial transcript I am totally convinced of his innocence. The Council he received during his trial was reprehensible. Woody, the name to which you all have gotten to know him was railroaded, simply because he had a relationship with the young victim.

No motive, no weapon, only the fact that he had been with her on the evening before she was killed brought a guilty verdict and a sentence of death. This whole case against Woody was so ill conceived and prosecuted that I couldn't believe my eyes when I read the transcript". He paused dramatically and let the crowd yell.

"I was so incensed I knew I had to reopen his case; such incompetents.

The whole trial should be dismissed on the grounds of stupidity. Everyone who took part in the investigation and prosecution should go back to school, I say."

"Careful, Mr. fancy lawyer. Let's not offend these good lawmakers. They could turn on us," Max warned but only to my ears.

"If it were not for the good work of a few, namely, Rev. Harley Daniels, Shapely Shaw and a wonderful journalist, Max Holmes, an innocent man would have been put to death. These wonderful, unselfish people have donated their time because they believed in Woody's innocence. As I speak, tests are being done on a switchblade knife they found hidden at the scene of the crime.

"I am certain this evidence will clear my client, Woodrow Howard Pierce of any wrong doing and will ensure he is released, a free man." He stood for moments after his speech to allow pictures to be snapped.

"More reporters are jumping on your bandwagon," I said to Max. That's all right. I will be first to get the results when they are released. Manos is taking care of everything." He leaned back in his chair and propped his feet on an ottoman in a relaxed manner.

Chapter Twenty-four

Max received the news and formally-by email. Carrie's blood residue was on the knife, still caked within the part of the knife where it folded together and clearly defined fingerprints marred the handle. He yelled the news to us all. Shapely, Howard and I rose from our chairs and did our happy dance. We had learned it was a great stress reliever and a good celebration tool. After singing Shapely's song, it became our dance tune. We sang as we jumped about to, Hey Little Liza, Little Liza Jane.

Max couldn't participate. He anxiously began writing his piece. I saw him spell **exclusive** in large type. What a story he was telling. I crossed my heart and said a small prayer. So far there had been no mention of Manos or his men. Other reporters were trying to get in on the story but that was part of Eric's job now.

When he saw a news badge or a camera in the club he did what he did best-bounce. Manos and his people were laying low.

The announcement of the new evidence took the media by storm. Max was riding high on all the publicity and so was Shapely. Howard, assuming that the danger to Shapely was no longer an issue decided to go home to share the rewards of the news with Summer.

Finally, Mr. Martin summoned Max, Shapely and me to Frankfort. The Governor was going to make a speech and requested our presence along with Summer, Woody's mother. Something was up and it had to be good news. Was it possible that our actions had procured Woody's freedom? A feeling of joy mixed with apprehension consumed me. I dared not hope for the ultimate goal of Woody's release.

Mr. Martin was evidently a good lawyer, he bragged he never lost a case. He was adamant in Woody's defense after the fact. Our hope was that he had succeeded again.

I had packed my bags. The investigation was over. It was out of our hands now. I took a long look around the apartment. Shapely had been a good hostess. In spite of the circumstance, I had enjoyed my time here. Max and Howard were hesitating also. We had all become friends and knew we would keep in touch when this was ended. Beth would be waiting for me in Frankfort. She and my parents had driven eastward last night and spent the

night in a hotel. My heart jumped at the thought of seeing and holding her again; maybe tonight would be like a second honeymoon. The news conference was being held at the entrance to the state capital building. The backdrop was tall stately pillars and walls made of Indiana Bedford limestone and Vermont granite. The sun was shining from a spectacular blue sky. The temperature was a perfect 70's.

A podium had been set up with many mikes attached. A dozen chairs lined the area behind, where we would sit. We numbered six, Summer, Shapely, Max, Howard and his daughter Cindy who was visiting, and me. A number of reporters stood on the first wide step where they could get good photos. We took our seats. Summer was smiling but shaking with nerves. My heart went out to her. This had to be good news. We waited, then at the appointed time the governor walked through the capital doorway. He held a sheaf of papers. He was accompanied by the attorney, Roberto Martin. Both were well-dressed and wore solemn expressions.

The governor took the microphone with Mr. Martin by his side. He spoke, "Ladies and gentlemen, I called this news conference today to share some wonderful information. Wonderful news for many who have joined us here today.

An application has been presented to the court by Mr. Roberto Martin, attorney at law, a motion to set aside the

conviction of Woodrow Howard Pierce, who was tried and convicted in a court of law for the crimes of rape and murder."

Summer gasped and clapped her hand over her mouth; the rest of us sat in silence.

"In very limited circumstances the court will entertain the motion especially if new exonerating evidence has been presented. In the case against Woodrow Howard Pierce, new evidence has been presented that without a doubt, exonerates Mr. Pierce. There are many people who have worked tirelessly to bring this case to the attention of the court and myself, many who believed in his innocence." He held up a stack of papers. "There are over 5000 names on this petition presented to me from different states.

All were made aware of this case by a writer, Maxwell Holmes, who is with us today." The governor raised his arm toward Max. Max stood and lifted his hand for recognition. For once, he was the subject of snapping cameras.

The governor then turned to Shapely and me.

"Two others who believed in Woodrow, worked tirelessly to prove his innocence." He laughed, "May I present, Shapely Shaw and Rev. Harley Daniels, known to you as the preacher and stripper, whose every struggle was documented by writer, Maxwell Holmes."

When we stood, everyone in the crowd began clapping their hands. I was overwhelmed. Shapely seemed as affected as I. For once she was dressed modestly in a pale blue suit, although it
was cut to flatter. We humbly bowed and lifted our hands to the crowd then took our seats. Within the applause I heard a definite voice call out, 'Yeah Harley.' It was Beth. I would know the sound of her voice in any circumstance.

"Under the expert presentation of compelling evidence by attorney Roberto Martin, I am happy to announce the conviction of Woodrow Howard Pierce has been overturned. He is free. Kentucky will never knowingly imprison an innocent man. May I present to you Woodrow Howard Pierce." The governor turned. Stepping forward was Woodrow himself. He appeared slimmer and pale but the glow on his face was undeniable. His plaid shirt and jeans hung on his thin frame. Summer screamed and rushed to him and hugged him close.

The rest of us restrained our actions but tears of joy ran down Shapely's face and I wiped my own eyes.

Woody stood at the podium. He appeared overwhelmed and unsure of himself. The reporters waited expectantly. Obviously overcome with emotion he said, "This is not a dream, is it? I can hardly believe this has happened.

I'm free. I would like to thank everyone who believed in me. Who knew that I could never kill anyone least of all the girl I loved, Carrie." He turned and called all our names. "I am blessed, I know I have been blessed." He shook the attorney's hand. Thank you Mr. Martin, I'll be eternally grateful to you."

It was my pleasure," he returned and gave Woody an embrace. "Justice will prevail," he said loudly raising both his hands. Everyone applauded.

"That's it, folks," the governor said. "Let's let this free man go and enjoy his freedom." With that last statement he left the makeshift stage and returned to the capital building.

My eyes searched for Beth. My heart was tripping, then I saw her making her way through the crowd. I couldn't miss her fiery red hair glistening in the rays of the sun. I hardly noticed my mother and father who accompanied her. Next thing I knew she was in my arms. I clutched her so tightly I knew she was breathless. It seemed everyone was hugging someone. Finally we settled down for introductions. The news reporters had scattered. I lead Beth and my parents around to meet everyone. When she met Summer, Beth said, "You have a beautiful name." I smiled at my wife. She was being genuine. I realized my absorption in the project had made her react unnaturally before.

Mr. Martin excused himself but before he left, he pulled out a gift card. "There's a steakhouse down the road. Take everyone for a meal. Woody looks like he could handle at."

I started to refuse. "We can't accept that."

He held up his hand to silence my protest. "This is not from me but an unidentified benefactor."

I took the card, "Give the benefactor our thanks."

We all gathered around a long table in the steakhouse.

"I think it would be most appropriate for each of us to thank the Lord personally at this time." Woody's sat at the head of the table. "Woody, will you be first?" I asked.

He hesitated. "You all know I haven't been a praying man but I'll try. Lord, I humbly thank you for my freedom. Thank you for the ones who believed in me. I guess you loved me after all. My heart's not cold anymore and the big hole inside me isn't there anymore. I'm filled with a warm feeling and I think it's you, Lord,. I don't know how else to explain it.

So right now I'm the most thankful man in the world. Amen."

Around the table, each gave thanks but I thought none could match the emotion Woody expressed. When Howard's daughter Cindy spoke she said," I'm just so thankful I chose this time to visit my dad and be witness to and a part of this special occasion, and to be here in the beautiful hills of Kentucky."

She was seated opposite me and I noted her smile and how her eyes crinkled at the corners when she smiled. Always the eyes, I thought. Something familiar, realization hit me like a blow, stunning me. Could it be possible? Howard and Summer were sweethearts before her rape. I didn't dare mention my suspicion.

I leaned over to Max and asked, do you have the address of that company that analyzes DNA?

"Yes," he replied. "It's in my computer."

"May I have it?"

"Of course, after we eat."

"Thank you, Max." The DNA samples should be easy to collect, everyone was using straws. I had a hunch and I just had to be right.

Our meals arrived and we turned our attention to the food before us. Max rose and lifted his glass. "Before we eat, I would like to make a toast.

To Harley, and Shapely who as the preacher and the stripper are two of the bravest people I know and who made my career. I feel they will always be my best friends. Without them none of this would be possible." Everyone raised their glasses.

After he took his chair, Beth rose and pulled a paper from her pocket. She took a deep breath and unfolded the stationary. "I had intended to share this with Harley later but I think you all should hear. It's a letter from the Trinity way church. It's addressed to Our Dear Pastor, Harley Daniels. Please forgive our error in judgment. We have come to realize you needed to follow your convictions. That is what makes you a special pastor. We have followed your progress and rejoice with you and the results of your efforts. The parish is anxiously awaiting you and that we miss you. We will celebrate your return to the pulpit of Trinity Way Church.

The letter was signed by each of the 12 board members, plus." Beth hesitated to clear her throat and wiped her eyes. "This is the second page with the signatures of all the church members."

Everyone applauded. A lump rose in my throat but I managed to say, "I would be honored if all of you could attend my first sermon back in the church."

"Don't worry, Preacher." Howard said. "I'll see that we all are there. I'll take care of the expenses."

"Hey let's eat," Max said, "our food is getting cold."
No one was going to allow that to happen.

Chapter Twenty-five

Finally, Beth and I were home, back at the parsonage of the Trinity Way Church. The cottage was just as we left it. My papers still lay on my desk in the study. I had expected everything we owned to be packed in boxes and waiting.

"You know," Beth said as she came up behind me and slipped her arms around my waist. "We don't have to stay here; there are stacks of letters requesting your services - speaking engagements and pastoral positions."

I turned and held her close. "I think we belong here. Within me is a deep sense of belonging. Until Woody was freed I couldn't allow myself the luxury of settling in. I simply couldn't rest."

"I understand," she said. Her eyes misted. "I have something to show you." She hesitated and sighed.

From her pocket she lifted a stack of letters, bound together with a rubber band.

"What are these?" I asked.

"Letters from prisoners, requesting your assistance.

I thought about tossing them but knew I couldn't. I held the envelopes for moment while Beth waited nervously. "I'll give these to Max. There may be a story here. He's the real investigator." Beth smiled.

"I have a couple of days before Sunday's sermon. I'll have time to hold you and hold you," I said to my wife.

"We've been apart too long. I never want to be away from you again, ever."

"I don't want you to be away from me either," she whispered back. With her head on my shoulder we swayed back and forth in pure happiness.

Sunday dawned bright. Rays of sunshine streamed through the parsonage windows. Howard had called. They all had arrived safely and would be at the church. God was good and definitely worked in mysterious ways. I was privileged. I put on my robe and humbly walked from the rectory to the pulpit. I stood for a minute and stared out over the congregation, all the familiar faces, even Janice was looking at me expectantly. I relished the joy rushing through me. I saw Max and Shapely. She was dressed in a modest beige suit and her hair was pulled up atop her head.

She looked like a Baptist. The two of them sat close together. Howard rested with his arm around Summer.

Cindy and Woody sat on either side of them. Mom and Dad were there also. Dad gave me the thumbs up sign and Mom blew me a kiss.

"It is so good to be home," I said, my voice resounding in the crowded room. Everyone rose to their feet and began applauding. For a long moment they clapped excitedly then sat back down on the pews.

"I have missed being here with you but the last two months have been most rewarding, exciting and frightful. I met wonderful people, who I feel, are now my extended family. I would like to introduce each one to you, my congregation."

"First is Woodrow Howard Pierce, the young man whom I met at the Eddyville prison, who convinced me he was an innocent man. I'm so glad I listened to my heart and God." Woody stood shyly for a moment then sat down. "Next, please meet Woody's mother, Summer Pierce." She followed Woody's example and stood briefly. Next, I introduced Howard and his daughter, Cindy. I explained how helpful and protective Howard had been. "Without these next two people, I'm afraid I could not have been successful in obtaining Woody's freedom. In a way you already know them so here they are in person. They both risked their lives to help me because they believed in righting a huge wrong.

First, Shapely Shaw, who was by my side through some dire situations." Shapely stood and a prolonged applause surrounded her.

"Thank you, thank you," she said.

"Maxwell Holmes is the writer who brought our struggles to you every week. His skill provided publicity that was crucial in obtaining Woody's release." Max stood and saluted with a big smile on his face. The congregation again broke out in applause.

"My experiences have taught me so much. I have come to realize that everyone has a purpose and a destiny. Trinity Way Church is my destiny, my love. To seek inspiration I need but look out over my congregation. I see faces exuding love, patience and strength. I see children of God and I am so thankful for you. Corinthians 9:15, Thanks be unto God for his unspeakable gift."

Chapter Twenty-six

My sermon was said. The congregation seemed pleased. I happily clasped each hand as they filed out of the church.

"Great sermon, Son," Dad said as he gave me a big hug.

Mom said, "We're so proud of you."

"Thanks," I returned, "remember, go to the parsonage for our little get- together."

Beth stood at my side. She looked up at me with love in her eyes. "I knew you could do it, Harley; you were wonderful."

"Will you escort our guests over to the parsonage?" I asked her.

"Of course." She motioned for Summer, Howard, Woody, Cindy, Max and Shapely to come with her. I smiled as Max took Shapely's hand. I would follow as soon as possible.

They were all gathered in the living room when I entered. My extended family, "I'm so happy you all came to hear my sermon." I said.

They all answered at once. " We were glad we could come." Happy to be here. Glad to share with you."

"I'll have to admit I had an ulterior motive for having you attend."

They all grew quiet and looked at me with expectant faces.

"What more can there be?" Woody asked incredulously. "You guys gave me back my life. I can never be more thankful."

"I think you might be," I said with a laugh, hardly containing the happiness bubbling up in me. "Here, I think the best way is to just let you read these reports." I pulled the folded papers from my breast pocket. "These are results from the DNA lab. I had a suspicion and followed through on it." I handed one to each, Woody, Summer, Howard and Cindy, then waited.

First, a sob broke from Summer and she sat down clutching her chest. Then Howard dropped beside her and took her in his arms. Woody stood as if in shock. For long seconds his handsome young face was frozen then he smiled and looked at Cindy who in turn stared at him. "You are my sister," he gasped.

She returned with a giggle. "And you are my brother." The two young people rushed into each other's arms and hugged tightly.

"I've always wanted a little sister," Woody choked.

"And I always wanted a big brother."

Max was busy snapping pictures. "I've got another story," he said. "What a great follow-up." Shapely was wiping her cheeks then blowing her nose.

Howard kept saying, "I can't believe it, I can't believe it." He held Summer's face in his hands. "We were so young and inexperienced, I wasn't sure we even. . . ." Summer placed her finger over his lips.

"Evidently we did, the night before . . . before the rape."

Woody threw his arms up into the air. "I have a family, a whole family, I have a dad."

Howard rose and grabbed Woody, "Oh, my son, my son." They held each other for a long time.

Finally everyone got control of their emotions. Woody came to me and shook my hand. "Rev, God is good, isn't He?"

"Yes," I replied. "God is good."

www.ingramcontent.com/pod-product-compliance
Lightning Source LLC
Chambersburg PA
CBHW061149170626
46809CB00003B/1032